DEATH CRAWLERS

GERRY GRIFFITHS

D1379809

SEVERED PRESS
Hobart Tasmania

DEATH CRAWLERS

WWW.SEVEREDPRESS.COM

This novel is a work of fiction. Names, characters, places and incidents
are the product of the author's imagination, or are used fictitiously.
Any resemblance to actual events, locales or persons,
living or dead, is purely coincidental.

ISBN: 978-1-925597-10-3

CHAPTER ONE

Derek Matlin and his wife, Tammy, were about to turn in for the night when the first marauder snuck into their camp. It climbed stealthily up the side of a tree and crouched in the overhanging branches that stretched out over the campsite. The young couple was none the wiser and had no idea that they were being spied upon.

Derek used a long stick and poked the ashes in the campfire pit. A few embers glowed orange. He took a small pail of water and doused them, creating a short-lived rise of smoke.

Another intruder crept behind a nearby bush. Two more were skulking behind the Matlin's two-person dome tent.

Tammy was inside, sitting on the ground tarp, pulling on a pair of sweatpants to sleep in as the park ranger had told them that the nights could get rather chilly. Tonight was the first in a three-day stay at the campground. They had been planning the trip for a few months and almost didn't come when they heard about the big fire that had decimated over two hundred acres of forest.

Toby, their wirehair terrier-mix, was lying on his back on top of Derek's sleeping bag, expecting a tummy rub from Tammy. He had one of her socks in his mouth.

"Give me that." Tammy grabbed the toe of the sock. Toby thought it was a game of tug-a-war and snarled playfully, shaking his head back and forth.

"Cut that out, you better not put a hole in it," Tammy said and pulled the sock out of Toby's mouth. "Now look what you've done, you made it all wet."

Toby gave her one of his sad adorable faces.

"Oh quit that. All right, you're forgiven."

But instead of jumping up and lapping her face, Toby's ears perked up. He immediately flipped around onto his feet. A low guttural growl resonated in his throat.

"What is it, Toby?" She held onto his collar to prevent him from bolting out of the tent. "Derek!" she called out.

"Yeah," Derek answered, coming from the car after making sure it was locked.

"Is there something out there? Toby's acting strange."

Derek looked around their campsite. "I don't see anything." He walked over to the nearby service road that looped around the small campground. There were twenty other designated camping spots adjacent to the road but they were all unoccupied, and probably would be for the weekend due to the destructive forest fire.

He walked back to the front of the tent and gazed in through the opening. "Sorry, there's nothing out here but—"

Something scampered onto the picnic table.

"What the hell?"

Derek heard rustling in the bushes, but as he turned to the sound, the branches above him began to shake. He reached into his back pocket and took out his flashlight. He turned it on and shined upward.

Five pairs of eyes stared down in the glaring light.

Derek stepped away from the picnic table—now there were four of them rummaging through a cardboard box full of goodies—and slowly backed toward the tent.

He turned, and saw one of them race down the tree trunk, headfirst, and scamper across the campsite. Derek tried not to make any sudden movements and cautiously pivoted so that he could assess the situation. They were completely surrounded.

"Derek?"

"Quiet."

Toby let out a series of forceful barks.

The creatures hissed and chattered.

"Make Toby stop."

"Toby, be still," Tammy coaxed from inside the tent. The dog barked once more and stopped, but still kept the persistent low growl.

Derek counted maybe twenty in the trees, more on the ground.

He felt trapped like a wayward settler in a circled wagon train, surrounded by a fierce band of Indians.

A few were standing on their hind legs, baring their teeth to show who was in charge. They had to weigh at least twenty to thirty pounds. Derek wondered if they had been driven out of their natural habitat by the fire and congregated into a large group in order to survive.

Tammy poked her head out of the tent. "Oh my God, Derek. Are they attacking us?"

"Try and not to move. And whatever you do, don't let go of Toby." Derek's mind was reeling. The first thing he thought was maybe they were rabid, the way they were snarling and baring their teeth. Aggression was a definite sign of an animal stricken with hydrophobia. Or maybe they were just naturally vicious.

He had read somewhere that they could kill a dog once they'd lured it into a body of water. A better swimmer, the creature would lead the dog halfway across a stream or a pond, then it would double back around, climb onto the canine's shoulders, and drown the dog.

And now they were beginning to converge on the tent.

"Get away!" Derek yelled and shined his light in every direction in hopes of scaring them off, but they held their ground, some even advancing.

Even if he'd had his rifle, there were too many.

"Derek," Tammy cried. "What are we going to do?"

Suddenly, they heard the loud blare of a car horn and approaching engine as a blinding halogen spotlight lit up the campground like a phosphorus bomb.

The startled raccoons shielded their masked faces with their tiny hands. They screeched and scurried in all directions, some of them colliding into one another.

The sound grew even louder as the park ranger's truck sped up and came to a halt, skidding in the dirt. Dave Morley jumped out of the cab and blasted an air horn canister.

He chased after the masked bandits, repeatedly sounding the horn, like a football fan cheering his team after a touchdown.

The raccoons hightailed it into the night.

"I don't think they'll be coming back, at least not for a while," he said, walking back into the campsite.

"Thank you so much," Tammy said, climbing out of the tent. She had put Toby's leash on and had the loop around her wrist. The small dog puffed his chest and sat down at Tammy's stocking feet.

"Good you kept your dog restrained. They would have killed him for sure. Raccoons can be a mean bunch. I know. I've seen them go at each other in the dumpsters, fighting over a silly candy wrapper. They especially like dog food, so I'd keep it in your trunk at night. Your food, too."

Derek looked over at the mess on the picnic table. "Thanks for the tip."

"If you like, I'll keep tabs on you folks. I don't expect too many people showing up this weekend due to the fire."

"Too bad for them. Thanks again, for coming when you did," Derek said.

"Just doing my job," Dave said. "Well, you better get some sleep. Anymore trouble, you just holler."

"Oh, we will," Tammy said. "We'll be the first you hear."

Dave grinned, gave the air horn another quick little blast, and went to his truck. He backed up onto the service road, and headed off to the ranger station.

Tammy led Toby back inside the tent.

Derek took a moment and panned the flashlight around their campsite just to be sure the raccoons were gone. He flicked off the torch, took a couple steps, and switched it back on. He shined the light around the campsite one more time.

"Good, now for some peace and quiet," he said, turning off the light and crawling into the tent.

***

Dave parked his truck and went inside the ranger station. It was a small building, and rustic inside. The walls were a dark wood panel with hanging pictures of photographs of the forest. A wood-burning stove was in one corner with a black smokestack stretching up into the ceiling. A long counter with a glass top and front sectioned off the room. Inside the display were literature about the national park, and old Indian relics.

Behind the counter was Dave's office area, his desk with a computer, and file cabinets. His short-wave radio was on a nearby table along with a copy machine.

He took off his ranger hat and was going to hang it on the coat rack when he heard a droning sound outside.

He went out on the porch and looked up at the night sky. There were a lot of stars, so it took him a second before he saw the moving lights. He could tell that the plane was moving away by the position of the red port light on the one wingtip and the green starboard light on the opposite wingtip.

It had to be at least five miles away, but it was difficult to be sure as he had no idea what type of plane it was, or how big, though he was pretty certain that it was one of those propeller jobs.

Suddenly, the sound of the distant engine died. The navigation lights dipped and plummeted into the distant treetops. He could hear the faint crash, the snapping of timber.

He rushed back inside and called it in.

CHAPTER TWO

"Has anyone seen my badge?" Wanda Rafferty called down the hallway.

Ally, her teenage daughter, yelled from her room, "No, Mom."

"Not a clue," Ryan said, stepping out of his room. Her oldest son went into the bathroom and closed the door.

"Dilly? Did you take my badge?" Wanda shouted as she came out of her bedroom.

She had on her typical working attire: official sheriff's ball cap, starched brown uniform shirt, blue jeans, and hiking boots. A black belt was snug around her slim waist holding a pair of handcuffs, a small can of Mace, two extra clips of ammunition, and her holstered Browning nine-millimeter pistol.

Even though the crows feet creased her temples and she had to pluck the occasional grew hair, she was still striking at forty. A long auburn ponytail stuck out the back of her cap.

She started down the stairs. "Dilly! I can't leave the house without my badge."

Wanda crossed the living room and stopped at the downstairs bedroom door. She knocked once and opened the door. As always, Dillon's room looked like the Looney Tunes Tasmanian Devil had performed his spinning cyclone and sent everything a jumble.

She saw the lump under the blanket. "Well, I guess if I can't go to work then poor Dilly wouldn't be getting any ice cream after dinner."

Wanda reached down and pulled up the blanket. Dillon's one-year-old bulldog, Rochelle, was fast asleep, snoring and leaving wet slobber on the pillowcase.

"Hold on there, partner," came a voice from across the room.

She saw a shadow standing behind the three-foot-tall Yosemite Sam cardboard cutout in the corner. Wanda's five-star badge was pinned on the cartoon character's chest in between both sides of his droopy mustache.

"You better come out before I shoot," Wanda said playfully.

Six-year-old Dillon stepped out from behind the cardboard cutout with his hands in the air. "I surrender."

"You bet you do." Wanda smiled.

Dillon unstuck the badge, brought it over, and handed it to his mother.

"Don't be taking things that don't belong to you." Then she added like a cowpoke, "You hear!"

"Yessum."

"And pick up your room. Breakfast will be ready in a few."

Wanda pinned on her badge and went into the country-style kitchen to start the coffee maker. Standing in front of the kitchen sink, she stared out the window. A long gravel driveway stretched out to the main road. A field of tall grass was on the other side.

She loved living in the farmhouse even though she knew nothing about agriculture or animal husbandry. She enjoyed the peacefulness of being out in the country. Her children, on the other hand, weren't as thrilled about the seclusion and often vented that they were bored and wanted to spend more time with their friends.

She had just poured her coffee when Ally screamed bloody murder.

Wanda put down her cup, sloshing some of the coffee over the rim and onto the cuff of her shirtsleeve. "Damn, what now?"

She rushed into the living room.

Ally was in her bathrobe and slippers, and was doing a nervous dance.

Dillon was playfully shoving a jar at his older sister.

"Mom, make him stop!"

"Dillon, quit teasing your sister."

"It's just a little spider."

Wanda marched up to her son and was ready to snatch the jar out of his hand when she saw what was inside.

It was the biggest and hairiest tarantula she had ever seen.

"Where'd you get that?" she said, backing away.

"Found it in the field. Isn't it beautiful?"

"Get that thing out of the house!"

Ryan came down the stairs. "What's all the ruckus?"

A white blur raced down the steps past him.

"Uh-oh. Now you've got Winston riled up," Ryan laughed.

The white bull terrier got caught up in all the excitement and jumped up on Ally's legs thinking that she was the cause of all the commotion and rightfully so.

"Winston, get down!"

He tore around to the front of the couch and plowed into Dillon. The boy stumbled back and dropped the jar on the hardwood floor. The jar smashed and broken glass went everywhere.

Dillon jumped up on the couch in his bare feet.

"Winston, get back," Ally said, hoping to ward the dog away from the sharp glass.

But Winston was too preoccupied eyeing the black thing scurrying onto the throw rug by the fireplace.

The tenacious dog sprang and knocked over the brass stand holding the fireplace tools. The long-handled broom, poker, and shovel clamored on the hearth brickwork.

Rochelle strolled out of Dillon's room to see what was going on. She was still sleepy and flopped down on the threshold to watch the fun.

The tarantula was fast and moved across the floor in short bursts then hopped in the air, making a landing then taking off again in a quick burst of speed.

It was almost to the front door where Ryan was waiting for it.

He quickly opened the door, and the cause of the morning mayhem ran out onto the porch and disappeared down the steps.

Ryan shut the door and smiled at his mother, sister, and brother. "So, what's for breakfast?"

CHAPTER THREE

Beau Tompkins had been following the same set of tracks for most of the morning when he realized he had ventured into a tract of the forest that he had never been before.

The impressions stopped at the edge of a small clearing.

He raised his Weatherby .308 and looked down the sight, hoping to see a large rack on a big buck but instead saw the twisted wreckage of an airplane.

The fuselage was mangled, having crashed through the thick timber. A broken-off blade from one of the propellers was impaled in a tree trunk. The nose was squashed. Both wings had been sheared off and were wedged against the crumpled tail section.

Busted wooden crates were scattered, having been ripped from the cargo hold.

Beau cradled his deer rifle in the crook of his arm. Soft loam and dead leaves meshed under his boots as he stepped into the clearing.

He stopped for a second and listened for any signs of life. Normally, the forest would be bustling with insect noises and chirping birds.

Everything was dead quiet.

He approached the crumpled cockpit. The windshield was smashed and the remaining side door was askew, hanging on one hinge.

Beau peered through the shattered glass and saw the pilot's lifeless body slumped facedown over the controls. The gauges on the instrument panel were splattered with grisly pulp and dried blood.

He heard a helicopter steadily approaching and stood in the middle of the clearing. The underbelly of the whirlybird came into view and hovered fifty feet above his head. He shielded his eyes as the downward draft kicked up loose dirt and leaves, and spun the debris around him as though he was standing in the middle of a swirling dust devil.

He yelled up to get their attention even though he knew they couldn't hear him over the din of the whirling blades. There didn't seem to be enough clearance between the trees for them to land.

As if reading his mind, the helicopter rose, banked over the treetops, and disappeared out of sight.

Beau figured they were reporting the location of the crash site and summoning a rescue team. There was no telling how long that would take. He didn't see any point in hanging around. He took out his compass, got his bearings, and headed back through the trees.

He'd been hiking through the shrub oak for about ten minutes when he came upon a worn path likely created by migrating deer and large predators. The trail dipped down into the brush.

Beau decided to take a smoke break and sat on a log. He leaned his rifle down and plucked a cigarette from the pack in his orange field vest and lit it with a lighter.

He gazed dreamily at the terrain, puffing on his cigarette.

Finishing his last drag, he dropped the butt and crushed it with the heel of his boot.

He heard skittering inside the log, and out of curiosity, scooted over to the end. He got on his knees, leaned down, and peered inside.

The fallen tree was somewhat hollowed from rot and was dark inside except for a small patch of light visible at the other end.

He took out his lighter and flicked the wheel.

An ineffective glow cast on the decaying wood. He extended his arm farther inside the log.

His thumb slipped off the wheel and he burned himself.

"Jesus!"

Something incredibly strong clamped onto his wrist and wrapped around his arm.

He dropped the lighter and tried to pull free, but whatever had hold of him was anchored and refused to let go.

His shoulder rammed up against the opening, the jagged edge of wood bruising his ribs and scratching his neck.

His arm felt like it was being crushed in a vise.

The thing continued to squeeze, reminding him of the time a nurse had over-inflated the cuff while taking his blood pressure and how it had hurt like hell.

He yelled when the damn thing bit him.

Like two red-hot nails driven into his wrist.

His skin crawled as though an army of fire ants was marching under his flesh followed by a nauseating wave that coursed through his body. His heart pounded, ready to explode.

Beau's tongue swelled like a potato wedged in his gullet. With the air cut off from his lungs, he quickly passed out.

Never knowing what killed him.

***

Derek and Tammy were taking Toby for a walk down a forest trail when they heard a loud roar from above. A high wind buffeted the treetops. Pine needles rained down on their heads. They ducked as a few pinecones fell and landed by their feet and bounced off the hard dirt.

"What is that sound?" Tammy yelled so that she could be heard over the din.

Toby ran around in a circle, barking and tugging on his leash.

Derek went to a spot where there was a break in the treetops and glanced up. "Holy cow, will you look at that!"

Two enormous twin-engine helicopters with orange fuselages were passing overhead. Erickson Air Crane was stenciled on each tail section. Derek had never seen anything like it. A mangled plane was suspended under the belly of the first helicopter.

The second whirlybird carried a netted cargo of shipping crates and other sections of the wreckage.

Crewmen wearing orange flight suits stood in the open hatchways on the sides of the aircraft and were pulling up ropes and chains dangling beneath the choppers. Seeing how the forest was so dense in areas, Derek figured that the salvage crew must have rappelled down and attached the chains so that the debris could be lifted into the air.

The main rotors were seventy feet in diameter, large enough to blot the sky with their spinning blades.

"Man, you don't see that every day," Derek said after the helicopters had flown by and disappeared over the ridge.

Tammy jiggled a finger in her ear. "I think I just went deaf."

"Let's get back. I'm getting hungry." Derek looked down at Toby. "How about you, boy?"

Toby looked up and barked.

"See, we had a little excitement."

"I thought you were Mister-I-Gotta-Have-My-Peace-And-Quiet," Tammy said.

"I'll show you a little peace and quiet," Derek replied and pinched Tammy's fanny.

"Oh, you're going to get it."

"I hope so."

CHAPTER FOUR

Jake Carver stood on the service station island and watched the semi-truck barreling by on Highway 50 as he pumped gas into his '85 Ford Bronco. He was dressed for the rugged outdoors, heavy parka, jeans, and hiking boots.

The front door of the gas station's convenience store opened and out rushed Jake's petite but tomboyish wife, Nora, with her pixy haircut. She was also dressed for the wilderness.

"I got you something," she hollered. She ran up onto the cement island and playfully bumped into Jake.

"Watch where you're going," he said.

"Take that!" Nora flogged Jake with a Slim Jim.

"Hey!"

"Don't be a wuss."

"Okay, bully-girl," Jake said. "What's got you all wound up?"

"Oh, I don't know." Nora tore the end off the wrapper, pulled out the thin sausage stick, and took a bite.

"I thought that was for me."

"You can share." Nora broke off a piece and handed it to Jake.

"Yours is bigger."

"Tough."

Jake took a deep breath. "Smell that mountain air."

Nora wrinkled her nose and said, "All I smell is diesel."

"That's 'cause you're standing next to the pump, silly."

The trigger on the nozzle kicked off on the filler hose. "That's weird. I gave Craig forty bucks to fill it up and it stopped at thirty," Jake said, staring at the gauge on the pump.

"Are you sure?"

"Yeah, I'm sure. I really wish you hadn't invited them along. I mean I like Gail and all, but Craig's such a pain in the ass."

"Jake, please. She's my best friend."

"I know. But he's such a jerk. How Gail puts up with his shit, I'll never know."

"Promise me you'll be nice. I really want us to have fun."

Jake took a bite out of his portion of the meat stick. "Think the Donner Party had Slim Jims?"

"You're terrible." Nora stood on her tiptoes and gave Jake a kiss.

"Here they come," Jake said, gazing over Nora's shoulder.

Craig Porter, stocky with a short buzz cut, bolted out of the store. The door was about to swing close and almost slammed into Gail as she tried to come out. Even though Gail was a little pudgy, she was still attractive. She and Craig looked like a couple of fashion models straight out of a Land's End catalogue.

"Hey, you two! Get a room!" Craig yelled.

"Craig, leave them alone," Gail said, dashing after her husband. She caught up and they sauntered over to the Bronco.

"It must be my lucky day," Craig boasted.

"Why's that?" Jake asked.

"Bought myself some Scratchers. Won sixty bucks!" Craig flashed the money for everyone to see.

"You would have thought he'd won a million bucks the way he was carrying on in there," Gail said.

"Hey, it's money, isn't it? I didn't see you win anything," Craig protested.

"I could have used that money in the tank," Jake said.

Craig ignored Jake and pocketed the money. He climbed up into the back seat of the Bronco, not bothering to wait for his wife. Gail shrugged and shot Jake and Nora an apologetic look before getting into the vehicle.

"Can you believe the nerve of that guy," Jake whispered to Nora. "Uses my money and doesn't even offer to split the winnings."

"That's Craig."

They got into the Bronco and drove off.

***

The Bronco followed the two-lane road through the Alpine forest.

"We just passed Kyburz, so it shouldn't be far," Nora said as she checked the map.

Jake suddenly slowed the vehicle. "Oh, no," he said.

Craig and Gail leaned forward between the front bucket seats to get a better view out the windshield.

"What the hell happened here?" Craig asked.

A dirt service road wound up a hill. The terrain on both sides was scorched from a recent firestorm. Boulders were charred black and the ground was covered with gray ash. The few trees left standing were skeletal stalks.

"I never heard anything about a fire," Jake said. "Did you, Nora?"

"No."

"So we came all this way for nothing. Isn't that just great," Craig said.

"Craig, they didn't know," Gail said.

"We should keep going."

"What for? I've seen enough."

"It's still eight miles to Williams Lake," Jake said. "Can't hurt to check."

"I'm game," Nora said.

"Count me in," Gail said.

Craig frowned and shook his head. "Waste of time if you ask me."

The Bronco drove up the hill through the barren landscape.

Nora stared out the window. "What do you think started it?"

"Lightning strike most likely," Jake said.

"More like some stupid ass with a cigarette," Craig said.

"Shame," Gail said. "I bet it was beautiful."

Nora turned in her seat and faced Gail. "We were up here a couple of years ago. It's gorgeous in the summertime."

"Yeah, I can tell," Craig said.

"Everyone cross your fingers," Jake said. "We're coming up on another hill." He gunned the four-wheeler up the steep road.

The Bronco reached the summit and stopped on a firebreak overlooking the road beyond as it dipped down into a lush green valley with tall ponderosa pines and Sierra junipers.

Farther below, grassy meadows and pebbled beaches surrounded a crystal blue lake.

Jake drove over the ridge while Nora pointed out the window.

"Welcome to Williams Lake," she said.

"So I take it you guys have never been up here before?" Jake asked.

"This is our first time," Gail said.

"We pick up the trail on the other side of the lake," Jake said. "It'll take us right into Desolation National Park."

"Is it a big park?"

"Oh, yeah. Over a hundred square miles."

"Aren't you afraid of getting lost?" Gail asked.

"No," Nora said, "we know the terrain, and Jake has a map of the area, plus he has his GPS. There's nothing to worry about."

"Well, that's good. I get lost just going downtown."

"So, Craig," Jake said. "Did you bring your rod?"

"My what?"

"Fishing pole. They got the best fishing up here. There's German brown, rainbow—"

"I hate fish!"

Jake smiled to himself. "Sorry to hear that."

CHAPTER FIVE

Wanda looked up from the paperwork on her desk when Deputy Arness Monroe rapped on her door.

"There's someone here to see you."

She gazed over her deputy's shoulder and saw a rugged-looking man in his mid-thirties standing in the main office. "What does he want?"

"Has questions about that plane."

"Show him in," Wanda said. She collected the papers in a tidy stack and tossed them back in her in-box.

Monroe escorted the man into her office and returned to his duties.

Wanda stood and offered her hand. "Hello. I'm Sheriff Wanda Rafferty."

"Frank Travis," he replied and grasped her hand.

He had a strong grip.

So did she. She could see it in his eyes that he was surprised, maybe even impressed. "Please have a seat," she said and sat in her swivel chair.

Frank occupied the chair positioned in front of her desk.

"How may I help you?" Wanda asked.

"I'm here about that plane that crashed not too far from here."

"Shouldn't you be talking to the NTSB?"

"They've been somewhat reluctant in releasing any information. Not until there's been a full investigation."

"Guess you'll just have to wait and see what they find. I'm sorry. What is it that you do?" Wanda asked.

"I'm an entomologist."

"You make a living catching bugs."

"Well, when you put it that way, yes. The pilot who died was a colleague of mine. Professor Raymond Trodderman."

"I'm sorry to hear that."

"Actually, he was more of a mentor. Brilliant man. He'd written countless papers and was credited for finding the rarest of creatures. I imagine there were more. He wasn't a man to brag, just loved his profession. Entomologists are a funny bunch. There are some that would do anything to make a name for themselves."

"What, so that they can get a silly bug named after them?"

"Don't scoff. No, seriously, I don't believe there's anywhere he hadn't traveled. He'd been in the Congo, all through the Amazon jungles, just about everywhere in Asia."

"He sounds like a regular Indiana Jones."

"Well, Jones was an archaeologist."

"Oh, yeah."

"I once went with him to Antarctica."

"You mean there's insects that can actually survive that cold?"

"Sure. The Antarctic midge. In fact, they can only tolerate freezing temperatures. Any warmer and they die."

"Fascinating," Wanda said, her tone a little condescending.

"Anyway, before his plane went down, Raymond sent me an email saying he was flying up from South America and that it was urgent that we meet."

"Do you have any idea why?"

"Only that he had made a major discovery."

"So why are you here?"

"I was hoping you could take me out to the crash site."

"Mr. Travis, is it?"

"Frank."

"Frank, I am rather busy." Wanda waved for Monroe to come into her office.

"Yes, Sheriff?"

"Any word from Beth Tompkins?"

"Beau still hasn't come home."

"Keep me posted if there's any news."

"Sure thing."

Wanda waited until Monroe had left then looked at Frank and said, "One of our locals is unaccounted for. We've combed the area where he normally hunts, but so far, nothing."

"How long has he been missing?"

"Couple days."

"Around the time Raymond's plane went down."

CHAPTER SIX

Jake parked the Bronco on the macadam in front of the ranger's station and the two couples climbed out.

"Craig and I will go in and get our wilderness permits," Jake said.

"Why do we need permits?" Craig asked.

"Two reasons. One if we want a campfire, the other so they can keep track of who is hiking in the park. We check out with the ranger when we return, that way they know we got out safely."

"And if we don't show up, what then?" asked Gail.

"They send out a search party."

"I can take care of myself," Craig said.

"Come on," Jake said. "Let's go check in."

Jake and Craig entered the ranger's station while the women waited by the Bronco.

Nora lowered the rear window, reached in, and took two bottled waters out of the cooler. She handed a drink to Gail.

"Thanks," Gail said. She glanced over at the campground. There were no other vehicles around except for a car parked in a campsite farther up the road. "This place must be a well-kept secret," she said, opening her water and taking a swig.

"Maybe they think the park's closed because of the fire," Nora said.

"Could be."

"So how are you feeling?" Nora asked.

"I'm okay."

"I worry about you."

"That's sweet. I finally told Craig."

"How did he take it?"

"I don't know. When I told him what the doctor said, Craig didn't seem that concerned, even acted indifferent to me. I had a sense that it was more of an inconvenience for him thinking that I may become a burden."

"Thank God they caught it when they did," Nora said.

"I'm not looking forward to being laid up after surgery. That's one reason I wanted to go on this trip. That and—" Gail started to tear up.

Nora put her arm around her friend. "Come on, sweetie, don't cry."

"I often wonder if he really loves me. Since I told him about the cancer, he won't even kiss me; treats me like I'm contagious."

"He's just adjusting. He'll come around."

"My God, I feel like a leper."

"Give it time. It'll be fine. You'll see."

"I don't want to spoil your weekend."

"Don't be silly. We'll have fun. You'll see."

Gale smiled halfheartedly.

"See, you're feeling better already."

"You know, our business hasn't been doing so well," Gail confessed.

"Why not? What happened?"

Gail took a drink of her water. "Craig's not much of a businessman."

"If you want, I could help out," Nora said. "I mean I don't have my business degree yet, but I have a good grasp of the concepts."

"It's nice of you to offer, but I don't think Craig would go for it. Did I tell you we might have to take in my dad?"

"Why, he's not doing well?"

"No. He's getting to the point where he can't remember things. He nearly burned his house down last week. Left something on the stove and forgot to turn it off. I'm afraid he's getting Alzheimer's."

"I'm so sorry."

"Let's just say Craig's not overly excited about the whole arrangement."

"You poor thing."

Jake and Craig strolled out of the ranger's station.

"Promise you won't mention any of this to Craig," Gail said to Nora, keeping her voice low, so the men wouldn't hear what they were saying. "I don't want him to get upset and spoil everything. I just want for us to have a good time."

"I promise," Nora whispered.

Jake smiled as he approached the women. "Looks like we're all set."

They climbed back into the Bronco and proceeded up the dirt road.

***

Everyone gathered around the map spread open on the hood of the Bronco.

"This is a topography map," Jake said. "Shows the trails and the different elevations of Desolation National Park. We're right here at the trailhead."

"Why do we need a map if you have a GPS?" Craig asked.

"I'm just using this so I can show you and Gail the trails we'll be taking." Jake used a felt pen and drew their route on the map. "From here, we'll be hitting Grouse Lake, take a little rest break, and then Hemlock Lake. We'll continue up to Vista Lake and camp there for the night."

"You're not going to believe this place," Nora said.

"Yeah, it's ten thousand feet up so you can imagine the view," Jake said.

"My lord," Gail said. "Are we going to be able to breathe at that altitude?"

"The air's a little thin, but we'll be fine."

"Sunday, we'll come down the mountain and trek over to Twin Lakes, spend the night there," Jake said. He folded up the map and went around to the driver's window and tossed the map on the seat.

The group walked to the rear of the Bronco where the backpacks were laid out.

"Hope you like the packs I picked out for you," Jake said. "The guy I rented them from says they're top of the line. I think you'll find them fairly comfortable to wear as they have good side suspension straps and lumbar support."

"We do appreciate you doing that, Jake," Gail said. "We would have been lost if we had to pick out our own backpacks."

"Yeah, it cost me enough," Craig griped.

"Believe me, after you've carried these packs for awhile, that extra money will seem well worth it," Jake said.

Nora helped Gail on with her backpack.

"Oh, my, this *is* heavy!" Gail said.

Jake walked over, opened the top flap on Gail's pack, and peered inside. "No wonder. You need to distribute some of your weight to Craig."

Nora took a peek. "My gosh. What are you trying to do, kill Gail?" Nora said, frowning at her own bad choice of words.

"Okay, okay," Craig said.

Gail slipped off her pack and let it drop on the ground. Craig removed a one-burner cook stove, two propane canisters, a set of pots, and an army surplus shovel from Gail's pack. He opened his pack and took out a blue tarp, a length of cord, and a roll of all-purpose duct tape and switched the items in each pack. "There! Happy now?"

Everyone strapped on their backpacks and started up the trail.

CHAPTER SEVEN

Wanda took Frank in her Jeep, and after a short jaunt, they arrived at the entrance booth to Desolate National Park campground.

"Hey, Wanda," greeted Dave.

"How's business?"

"Slow right now."

Wanda motioned to her passenger. "This is Frank Travis."

Frank acknowledged the park ranger with a friendly nod.

"Please to meet you," said Dave.

"Frank, Dave Morley, our local park ranger."

"Hi, Dave."

"We're going to the crash site," Wanda said.

"Hope you brought your bug spray."

"See you later, Dave," Wanda said and drove into the campground. They passed a dozen unoccupied campsites before seeing any campers. A young couple sat at a picnic table with their small dog. At first, they looked concerned as the Jeep with the sheriff's logo on the door passed by, but then they recognized Wanda and were quickly put at ease when she smiled and waved and kept on going.

Eventually, they reached the last vacant campsite and the dirt road ended at the base of a hillock. A firebreak stretched up between the trees.

"How far is it from here?" Frank asked.

"After we get over that ridge, another two, three miles on foot." Wanda looked over at Frank. "I have to warn you, it's a little bumpy."

"Ever drive in the Amazon jungle?"

"No. I wouldn't go down there if you paid me."

"Oh, why's that? It's quite beautiful."

"I hate bugs," Wanda said.

"But they're remarkable creatures."

Wanda pointed to the scar over her left eyebrow; a zigzag indentation that looked like a lightning bolt. "Hobo spider. Little bastard. Thought I was going to die."

"I can relate. While on an exploration, a Brazilian wandering spider put me flat on my back for almost a week."

"So you know why I hate bugs."

"They're not all bad."

"If you say so." Wanda shifted into low gear and tromped on the gas pedal.

The four-wheel-drive Jeep bounced up the rutted firebreak.

While fighting the wheel, Wanda glanced over at her passenger.

Frank was holding onto the grab handle with a big smile on his face.

***

"They had to airlift the wreckage out of here," Wanda said as they walked into the clearing.

It was difficult to believe that it had been a crash site, as the only sign that there had been an event was the gouged earth and ruined trees, which could have resulted from an act of nature.

Wanda watched Frank roam the area, checking the ground, and then stopping to look up at the treetops flattened by the plane's descent. He knelt and picked up a handful of straw and showed it to Wanda.

"Packaging material." He studied it closely before slipping it into a large plastic bag and sliding the sealer. He tucked the bag in a side pocket on the daypack strapped over his shoulders. The worn lanyard grip of a bolo machete protruded out of a long sheath attached to the side of the rucksack.

He stood and closed his eyes.

"Not going to find much that way," Wanda commented.

"Close your eyes."

"What?"

"Humor me."

Wanda shut her eyes. Everything around her was absolutely still. "I don't hear anything." She opened her eyes and looked at Frank who was staring back at her.

"I know. Something's scared off the wildlife."

"Like what?"

"Let's scout around."

"We have about two hours then we're heading back. I don't want to be traipsing around in the dark."

"Fair enough."

CHAPTER EIGHT

Jake was in the lead as they hiked along the trail. Nora and Gail were next, with Craig taking up the rear. They traveled through an open meadow and were accosted by gnats and mosquitoes at the shoreline. Everyone broke out the bug spray.

Leaving the lake, they headed up a steep mountain path.

They traversed up a switchback and passed a sign: *DESOLATION NATIONAL PARK-PERMIT REQUIRED BEFORE ENTERING.*

Jake called out over his shoulder, "We're entering the park!"

They continued following the trail.

Jake stopped by a cascading stream. He reached along his belt and removed a stainless steel cup with a curved handle. "You guys have to try this." He dipped his cup into the fast-flowing water and took a drink.

"Jake's right, this is the best," Nora said. She scooped some water into a similar cup, took a sip, and passed the cup to Gail.

Gail drank down the rest. "Oh, that is good."

"Aren't you supposed to boil that first to kill the parasites?" Craig asked as he made a face.

"It should be okay," Jake said.

"Well, I'm not drinking it!"

"No one's forcing you to." Jake hooked his cup on his belt and they continued up the trail.

***

The four backpacks were propped against the trunk of a tree.

Nora and Gail were relaxing in the shade while the men explored the shoreline of Grouse Lake.

"It's so beautiful up here," Gail said as she took a sip from her canteen. She leaned back on her hands then suddenly jerked forward. "Oh my God, what was that?"

Nora glanced at the ground where Gail's hands had been. "It's a patty," she said.

"A what?"

Nora started to laugh. "You put your hand down on a cow patty."

"You mean—"

"Yeah, manure."

Gail immediately wiped her hand off on the grass. "What in God's name are cows doing all the way up here?"

"Don't ask me. They get up here somehow to graze." Nora stabbed the cow patty with a stick and held it up to show Gail.

"Almost looks like one of those bear claw pastries," Gail said.

"Want a bite?"

"Get it away!"

The cow patty snapped in two and ugly white maggots spilled out of the center.

"Oh, shit!" Gail said.

Nora tossed the cow patty into a bush. "Oh, shit is right."

"Maybe they should change the name of this place from Grouse Lake to Gross Lake."

Nora and Gail broke out laughing.

* * *

The hikers marched by Hemlock Lake with its surrounding rock formations and sparse stand of pine trees. The trail was wide enough for Nora and Gail to walk side by side so that they could talk.

"You know, I've never done anything as adventurous as this in all my life. I never dreamed I would be backpacking."

"Funny," Nora said. "You've always struck me as the outdoors type."

"Me? Hardly. I grew up in the city. My folks never were much for camping, that kind of thing."

"That's too bad. I don't mind roughing it once in awhile."

"Well, this is a great experience for me, let me tell you. I haven't felt this alive in years."

"You've been through a lot lately. You deserve to feel good about yourself."

"That I do," Gail said. "What's that?" She pointed to the large white patch ahead covering the trail. "Is that snow? It's the middle of summer for crying out loud."

"There's snow up here all year round because of the high elevation. Hope you remembered to bring some warm clothes."

CHAPTER NINE

"Jesus, what is that?" Wanda said.

The thing crawling between the leaves was at least twelve inches long.

Frank picked it up with his bare fingers. "*Scolopendra gigantea*: a giant Amazonian centipede. Which is the biggest in the world, and has no business being in this neck of the woods."

Wanda took a step forward to get a better look. "Creepy-looking insect."

"Well, actually, it not an insect. It's an arthropod. The body is segmented. See how the legs are smaller up front and get longer toward the tail."

"You're right."

"That's so they don't trip over their own feet," Frank laughed. "One thing you have to be careful of is the forcipules near the head. They act like fangs to inject a paralyzing venom."

"How poisonous are they?"

"A specimen this size kills birds and rodents."

"So this is what your friend wanted you to see?"

"I strongly doubt it." Frank reached up and pulled out a two-foot-long tube with perforated air holes from the daypack. He tucked the cylinder under his armpit and unscrewed the lid with his free hand. He dropped the large squirming centipede inside, twisted the lid close, and shoved the tube into the pack.

"What now?" Wanda asked.

"We keep looking."

They followed a crude trail through the forest.

Frank came to an abrupt stop and looked down at the ground.

Wanda saw what Frank was staring at. "I should have mentioned there are rattlers out here."

The entomologist reached down and picked up a long yellow husk, as fat around as Frank's forearm. He held it up shoulder height. The end just touched the ground. "This isn't snakeskin. It's from a centipede."

"Centipedes shed their skins?"

"Oh yeah."

"But that has to be over five feet long. I thought you said the one you caught earlier was the largest of its kind."

"Or so I thought. Must be another one that escaped from the plane." He looked concerned.

"What's wrong?"

"Normally after a centipede sheds its skin, it eats it."

"Are you serious?"

"It's a form of self-cannibalism."

"So why is the skin still here?"

"Must have found something better on the menu."

***

It was just after eight o'clock at night when they finally returned to Wanda's office. After freshening up in the washroom, she'd phoned in an order at the local Chinese restaurant and had the food delivered.

They decided to eat at her desk so Frank could plug in his laptop.

Frank dipped his chopsticks into a carton and slurped noodles into his mouth.

"I hope you don't mind. I like it a little spicy," Wanda said, taking a bite of Mongolian beef.

"This is nothing compared to some of the weird food I've eaten."

"Yeah, like what?"

"Cuy is quite popular in Peru and Argentina."

"And what is that?" Wanda asked, raising her chopsticks.

"Fried guinea pig."

Wanda dropped her sticks into her carton. "I had to ask."

Frank put his food down. "Did you know that centipedes have been occupying this planet for more than 400 million years?"

"Really, that long, huh?"

"Almost twice as long as the cockroach."

"Persistent little buggers," Wanda joked.

"If you're interested, I've downloaded some short videos on centipedes. There's one I think you will find fascinating of a large centipede hanging from a cave ceiling catching and eating a bat that it snatched out of the air." Frank pushed a key and turned his laptop around so that Wanda could see the screen.

"No, thank you," Wanda said and pushed the screen down flat onto the keyboard.

"Yeah, you're probably right."

"So, how dangerous are these things?"

"Judging by the size of that molt we found, I'd say extremely dangerous. I've estimated the toxicity levels based on data I have collected."

"And?"

"A creature this size could easily kill a person."

"So how many do you think there are?"

"There's no way of knowing. Not until I see the flight manifest."

"Which won't be until they've completed the investigation."

"In the meantime, maybe you could post warning signs around the area," Frank said.

"Hardly. There's over a hundred square miles of forest out there."

"Then I'll need to go out there again."

"Not in the dark you won't."

"Yeah. Any idea where I can stay tonight?"

"I have an empty cell in the back. The mattress isn't much."

"Believe me, I've slept in worse places."

Wanda went over and opened a metal cabinet. She took out a small bundle and handed it to Frank. "Here are some clean sheets."

"Thanks."

"Once you get situated, I have to get home to my kids."

"Isn't Mr. Rafferty there?"

"No. And there is no Mr. Rafferty."

"Guess I'll see you before sunup."

CHAPTER TEN

The four hikers stood on a granite ledge overlooking the valley below. The terrain was mostly terracing rock slabs and granite, with a few clusters of pine trees.

Beyond the valley were a spur and another mountain range.

"Almost takes your breath away," Nora said.

"I can't believe how desolate it is up here," Gail said.

"Like being marooned on another planet," Jake said.

"When do we eat?" was Craig's comment.

"So, you guys," Jake said. "What do you think of Vista Lake?" He turned around to present the small Alpine lake at the base of the amphitheater of rock.

"Amazing," Gail said.

Jake pointed to the summit one hundred feet up. "The peak's Mount Price. Means we're at ten thousand feet."

"I can't believe we climbed all this way," Gail said.

"I can," Craig said.

Gail reached in her pocket and offered Craig a granola bar. "Here, this should hold you over."

"Forget that. I want some real food," Craig said and pushed it away.

***

Nora emptied a packet of freeze-dried food into a boiling pot on the portable burner while Gail arranged the mess kits on a tarp.

Jake finished setting up his dome tent. He glanced over at Craig who was struggling to put up his tent.

"Need a hand?" Jake asked.

"I got it," Craig replied. He inserted a pole. The tent stood for exactly two seconds before it collapsed.

"I know. How about I put up your tent and you can find us some firewood?"

"Where'd you get this tent anyway? Damn thing's defective. What do I use to chop wood with?"

"Here, take this," Jake said, and tossed a hatchet, which landed a foot in front of Craig's feet. Craig picked up the short ax and headed toward the nearest stand of trees.

A few minutes later, both dome tents were set up, and Craig had built a rip-roaring fire in a pit formed out of rocks. He broke a branch in two and tossed the wood into the fire.

Jake stood over by the lake and was trying out his luck fishing. The tip of Jake's pole suddenly dipped and he began cranking the reel. He reached down and pulled a rainbow trout out of the water by its gills. He raised his catch in the air. "Hey, you guys! Who wants fish for dinner?"

Craig scowled at Jake.

Nora was excited for Jake and waved at her husband. "Way to go, honey!"

Gail clapped her hands as Jake took a bow.

"Jake seems to be enjoying himself." She glanced at her husband who was brooding by the fire. "Wish I could say as much for Craig."

"He'll feel better after we eat."

"Don't count on it."

CHAPTER ELEVEN

At dusk, the only leftover from dinner was a fish head in the skillet. Nora and Gail collected the dirty mess kits, the skillet, and the pots then trudged off toward the lake while Jake and Craig relaxed around the fire.

"You know what we need?" Craig said.

"What's that?" Jake asked.

"Some scotch!" Craig reached into his backpack and pulled out a fifth of whiskey. "Give me your cup."

Jake held out his empty coffee mug. Craig poured them both a stiff drink.

"We better not get too hammered," Jake said. "You don't want to feel like crap in the morning."

"Nonsense. Smoke?" Craig took two cigars out of his pack.

"Sorry, I'll pass," Jake said.

"Suit yourself." Craig grabbed a burning stick from the fire and lit his cigar. "Hey, check this out!" He reached back inside his pack and pulled out a large gun.

"Jesus, Craig! What the hell did you bring that for?"

Craig proudly showed off the weapon. "Ain't she a beaut? Forty-five-caliber Colt Combat Commander. Picked it up at the gun show."

"This is a national park. They don't allow guns."

"I have the right to protect myself, don't I? What if we meet up with a bear?"

"I doubt if that will happen. Just put it away."

"Okay, relax, you don't have to freak out."

"Just not a good idea, that's all," Jake said.

Craig stuffed the gun back into his pack just as the women came back from finishing their chores. Gail spotted the bottle of scotch. "What's a lady got to do around here to get a drink?"

Craig filled two more mugs and the four of them got cozy around the fire.

Gail gazed off into the horizon. "Are those lights?"

"The nearest town," Jake said. "It's about fifty miles away."

"I never dreamed we'd be this far away from civilization," Gail said.

"Hey, Gail," Nora said. "Want to see something cool?"

"Sure."

Nora activated the sleeve on her coat causing it to glow a bright lime-green, which gave off a surprising amount of light.

"How's that possible?"

"I'm not sure. Jake? What's it called again?"

"Electroluminescence. I have it too. Pretty trick, wouldn't you say?"

"I'll say," Gail said. "I'd love a coat like that. Wouldn't you, Craig?"

"I don't see the big deal when you've got a flashlight."

Craig poured another round of drinks.

"Now you know how the mountain men must have felt," Jake said. "Like that movie with Charlton Heston and Brian Keith."

"I think we saw that," Gail said.

The campfire began to hiss. Nora extended her hand out in front of her. "Don't tell me…"

"Great, rain. What's next?" Craig grumbled.

CHAPTER TWELVE

After a night of heavy rain, the twilight drive up the muddy firebreak was treacherous. Wanda and Frank left the Jeep on the rise and hiked into the forest. After more than an hour plodding through the woods, they reached the general area near the crash site and found the first dead animal, or what was left of it.

"My guess it was a raccoon," Frank surmised, as all of the flesh and soft tissue had been eaten, including the eyes and face.

"Are those holes in the fur?" asked Wanda.

"It appears that while the animal was paralyzed from the venom, its attacker burrowed in and out of its body while it ate it alive."

"And you think it could do that to a person?"

"Oh, yeah."

Something skittered beneath the fallen leaves by the base of a tree.

Wanda drew her nine-millimeter from the holster, took quick aim, and fired. The bullet rammed into an exposed root and exploded the wood.

A giant centipede raced out from under the groundcover. At first glance, it looked like an enormous slithering python. But then Wanda saw the scampering claw-like legs propelling the elongated exoskeleton body.

She fired off another shot, this time, blasting off two of its legs, which didn't slow it down.

"You're wasting your ammo," Frank said. "Shoot off a leg and it will just grow another the next time it molts." He pulled his machete out of its sheath and raced after the creature.

The centipede was extremely fast, but Frank proved faster. He grabbed the fleeing arthropod by its back legs, lifted a portion off the ground, and swung the machete, slicing its body in two. A greenish goop spurt out of each severed end and splashed on the ground. The bisected creature squirmed for a moment, and then was dead.

"A heart-like organ runs the length of the body." Frank raised his machete. "Best way to kill them."

"Really, it's that simple?"

"If that makes you sleep easier."

"Knowing these things are out here, hell no."

Frank insisted they continue their search in hopes of determining the number of gigantic centipedes on the loose.

After three hours of searching and finding other dead animals, some having been as large as a deer and a coyote, they came across the tenth victim.

This time, it was a fawn, breathing shallowly, being ingested by a centipede coiled around its frail body.

Wanda reached for her sidearm.

"Don't," Frank said.

"I'm sorry, but I can't just stand here and watch this."

"I know. But I want this one alive."

"What?"

"Give me a hand." Frank slipped his rucksack off his shoulders and laid it on the ground. He opened the top flap and pulled out a folded burlap bag.

"You're going to put it in there? Won't it chew its way out?"

"Not after I sedate it." He took a small plastic bottle and a rag from his bag, unscrewed the cap, and poured a tiny amount of liquid onto the cloth. "This should put it out for awhile."

After a few brief instructions, Frank interrupted the centipede from its feast—making sure that he had a firm grip just behind the head, clear of the paralyzing fangs—and held up the struggling creature while Wanda opened the burlap bag.

Frank held the chemical treated rag over the centipede's breathing membrane until it went limp and then he released it into the hemp sack.

"Heavy," Wanda commented, pulling the drawstring close.

"I'd say it weighs about ten pounds." He reached down, picked up his backpack, and slipped the strap over his shoulder. He took the burlap bag from Wanda and they walked on.

After a time of scouting the woods, Frank paused to locate their position on his GPS tracker and they headed in the direction where the Jeep was parked. Coming off a steep trail, Frank stopped to study a small patch of ground where the earth had been churned, forming a small cavity.

Wanda bent over and peered down.

A large centipede was coiled like a garden hose, its legs clinging to white spheres the size of pale vineyard grapes.

"My God, they're already breeding?"

"And at an accelerated rate, it seems. Which is rather strange as centipedes don't copulate."

"But how…"

"They're somewhat lazy when it comes to sex. The male simply finds a spot to unload his sperm and ambles off. It's up to the female to track down the spore bundle and keep the species going."

"How romantic."

"I'm afraid it's time for some family planning." Frank set out and came back, hefting a large rock with both hands.

***

Derek sat on his picnic table as a few campers straggled into the campground. The first vehicle was an older RV with the forward-sleeping compartment over the van's cab and looked like it had been all over the country; maybe several times. The paint on the aluminum siding was faded. The rim on the rear spare tire was all rusty. The windows were dirty. The relic looked like it hadn't been washed in ages.

Once they'd found a level spot, the driver turned off the engine. Soon, the side door opened and a three-stepper slid forward. A man in his sixties came out. He looked like it had been a while since he'd last bathed. He wore a wrinkly sweat-stained shirt and a rumpled pair of trousers.

He opened a side compartment and pulled out a rolled-up section of outdoor carpet and spread it out on the ground in front of the steps.

Derek could see a fat tabby stretched out on top of the dashboard, soaking up some sun.

The man looked Derek's way and gave him a wave.

Derek waved back.

It wasn't long before the man and his wife were sitting in a ratty pair of lawn chairs, drinking canned beer on the shabby carpet.

Twenty minutes later, another couple showed up, disrespecting the tranquility of the outdoors. They set up camp a few sites away, laughing loudly and blasting their boom box. Derek could smell weed coming from their direction.

He heard the zipper on the dome tent and saw Tammy climb out, almost tripping over Toby.

Toby ran up and leaped onto Derek's lap. "Hey, boy."

Tammy sat on the bench by Derek's feet and put her arm around his legs. She glanced over at the noisy couple.

"So much for peace and quiet," Derek said.

CHAPTER THIRTEEN

By the time Wanda and Frank reached the Jeep, it was late afternoon and the rain had returned. Wanda's uniform was drenched, her once-starched shirt clinging to her like a damp sheet. The notepad in her breast pocket was probably ruined, but at least she still had the ballpoint pen tucked in the booklet's spine.

She was weary from the long day. Frank was a tireless machine, accustomed to harsher conditions.

Wanda opened the driver's door. She pulled her boot free from the mud to step up into the seat, her other boot making a sucking sound as she slipped behind the wheel.

Frank got in on his side, tossing the rucksack on the floor, and putting the burlap bag behind the front seat.

"Jesus, it's really coming down," Wanda said as she started the engine and turned on the windshield wipers.

"I wouldn't exactly call this a monsoon," Frank said.

"I know: everything's bigger in the Amazon."

Frank smiled. "Apparently."

Wanda shifted into gear and steered down the slick embankment. The firebreak had turned into a perilous mudflow. The more Wanda tried to steer straight and regain traction, the more the ground beneath the tires shifted under the Jeep.

Frank glanced over his shoulder at the burlap bag. "Oh, no!"

"What?" Wanda said, looking at Frank.

"It's moving."

The tires on the left side suddenly sank into a deep rut. The vehicle flipped over, crashing down on the driver's side. Wanda's head slammed against the glass. Not having put on his seatbelt, Frank was thrown forward.

The Jeep slid down the muddy slope and edged out over an escarpment, plummeting thirty feet into a rocky ravine steadily filling with rain runoff.

***

Derek wore a poncho and made sure that the campsite was secure for the night and protected from the rain. The evening before, the band of marauding raccoons had made off with a good portion of their food on the picnic table, getting into the cereal and ripping apart boxes. They'd even licked the skewers clean that had been used for barbequing and roasting marshmallows.

The nocturnal scavengers had been bold enough to tip over the ice cooler and run off with most of its contents, forcing Derek to make a run into town to replenish their supplies. He wasn't taking any chances this time, having locked all the food inside the car's trunk as Ranger Morley had suggested.

He glanced over at the dome tent, the interior aglow by the battery-operated lantern and saw Tammy's silhouette moving about inside. The drawdown zipper was partially raised, enough space for Toby to squirm his way out and race over, dragging his leash in the wet dirt.

"Make sure Toby goes tinkle," Tammy said, poking her head out of the tent.

"Yes, ma'am."

"Keep that up and you'll be sharing a sleeping bag with Toby," admonished Tammy.

Derek gazed lovingly at his dog. He reached down, picked up the end of the soiled leash, and looped it around his wrist. "Hey, boy, looks like you and I might be bunkmates."

"Very funny," Tammy said. "And hurry back so you can warm me up, I'm freezing."

Derek shrugged and smiled.

Toby charged off, nearly yanking Derek's arm out of the socket. For being only twenty-five pounds, Toby was strong as an ox.

They ran down a slope in the dark. A couple times, Derek almost slipped trying to keep up with the sprinting dog.

Derek dug in his heels as they neared the restroom building.

He led Toby into the men's side of the lavatory. Derek could just make out the single sink and the two toilet stalls in the dark room as the overhead light bulb had gone out.

Derek saw three long strands hanging from the ceiling over the sink.

He hadn't remembered seeing sticky fly ribbons before.

Something was stuck to the adhesive of one of the strips.

Derek took a couple steps toward the sink.

Toby gave a cautionary growl.

"Quiet," Derek scolded.

The thing at the end of the strip thrashed.

"Whoa." Derek leaned in for a closer look.

The furry creature screeched, baring its tiny teeth as it flapped its wings frantically to get free.

"Must be some industrial strength..." Derek froze when he realized that it wasn't a fly strip, but a dangling creature with hundreds of legs.

Derek gasped when the predator's mandible jaws thrust into the bat's chest.

CHAPTER FOURTEEN

Wanda awoke to considerable pain.

The Jeep's body was crushed inward having landed between two massive boulders, pinning Wanda in her seat. Blood drizzled down the left side of her face, and she feared her cheekbone was fractured. She tried moving her left arm, but it hurt too much, so she stopped.

Her ribs ached from the shoulder harness that had cinched tight from the impact. She reached down to push the release button, but the locking mechanism was jammed. It was becoming increasingly difficult to breathe.

Rising water streamed in through an opening onto the floor mat.

She looked over and saw Frank wedged between the dashboard and the passenger seat. She could see where his head had struck the windshield. His hair was matted with blood. She wasn't sure if he was still alive.

Outside, the rain continued to drum the metal exterior of the Jeep, the water leaking through the cracked glass.

Motion caught her peripheral vision. She craned her neck to peer over her shoulder and saw the burlap sack on the back seat.

She heard a faint scratching sound, or was it—chewing?

The centipede poked its monstrous head out of the coarse fabric.

***

Derek dragged Toby and bolted out of the restroom. They ran down the path that led to the paved road. The campground was pitch dark except for the sprinkle of stars shining high above the treetops.

Rushing by, Derek hesitated when he saw the obnoxious man and woman inside their lighted tent, their silhouettes cast against the canvas. They were spinning around, screaming. Things that looked bizarrely like detached spines were clinging to their backs.

It reminded him of that old Vincent Price movie, *The Tingler*, they'd rented once on Netflix.

The woman collapsed, followed by the man who knocked over the light source.

Toby dashed off, pulling the leash out of Derek's hand.

"Toby, get back here!" Derek yelled, but the feisty dog was already gone.

Derek heard a bang and turned as the RV door flew open and the man dove out. He hit the ground and rolled in the dirt. He was desperately trying to shake off a spiraling creature twining around his leg.

Inside the camper, his wife yelled something and let out a God-awful scream like she was a banshee on fire.

Derek glanced over at the windshield of the van RV. Something hideous was wrapped around the cat, squeezing it in a death grip. The feline's eyes bulged. Blood sprayed the glass.

Derek darted into his campsite.

"Tammy!" he yelled. "We've got to get out of here!" He scurried over to the picnic table, and grabbed the propane camp stove. He carried it to the car, opened the trunk, and placed it inside next to the ice cooler and boxes of food.

He left the trunk open and raced to the dome tent. "Tammy, did you hear me? We have to go!"

He poked his head inside.

Toby stood by Tammy, who was on her knees, her back pressed against the curved wall of the tent.

"Why didn't you...?" and then he saw something moving inside one of the sleeping bags.

He stared in disbelief as it slowly crawled out.

"Jesus, Derek, what is that thing?"

Toby charged to protect Tammy.

"No!" Derek yelled.

The creature moved lightning-fast sensing it was under attack. Toby jumped on the thing with both front paws, pinning it to the ground and took a big bite out of the slithering body. Green liquid oozed onto the sleeping bag.

The injured creature retaliated and bit the dog's right front leg. Toby let out a whimper.

Derek immediately scampered on his hands and knees into the tent. He grabbed the battery-operated lantern and repeatedly slammed it down on the thing, crushing the body.

"They're everywhere." He grabbed Tammy's hand and pulled her out of the tent. Toby followed them, but after going only a few steps, he keeled over onto to the ground.

"Come on, boy, what's wrong?"

"Derek, what if that thing was poisonous?"

Derek lifted Toby. The dog went slack in his arms. "Hang in there, buddy."

Tammy hurried to the car. She opened the front passenger door and got in. Derek put Toby on her lap. He shut the door and jogged to the rear of the car.

He reached up to shut the trunk.

A creature raced out from the cargo compartment.

Derek slammed the trunk lid down, cutting the repulsive thing in two.

He jumped in the car, fired up the engine, and they sped away from the campsite.

They'd almost reached the main entrance when Tammy shouted, "Over there," pointing to the park ranger's truck parked by a storage shed.

"We have to warn him," Derek said. Tammy nodded in agreement as he pulled over and stopped. Climbing out of the car, he noticed the truck's door was open. He approached the cab and looked inside.

The park ranger was sprawled on the bench seat.

Derek gagged when a blood-soaked insectan head bore out of the man's stomach.

CHAPTER FIFTEEN

Wanda watched the giant centipede slowly crawl out of the burlap bag. One-inch long legs marched in unison over the back seat and down the front to prowl the carpeted floor, and still it hadn't completely exited the hemp sack.

She lowered her hand and reached for her gun. Her hand dipped into the cup of the empty holster. She strained to look around, but her semi-automatic was nowhere to be found.

Frank jerked and mumbled something.

"Frank. Wake up!" Wanda whispered, but he didn't stir.

She stared in horror as the centipede climbed up the backside of the console.

Wanda slowly raised her right hand and gripped the strap of her shoulder harness.

The antennae of the centipede brushed the wet fabric of her shirt. She could see the deadly venomous fangs protruding from the bulbous head.

Frank groaned.

The centipede turned its head, drawn to the sound.

Wanda looked over at Frank and noticed that his pant leg was torn, exposing a deep gash in his thigh. Glancing down at the floor, she saw the machete tucked between Frank's right boot and the doorframe. There was no way she would be able to reach the weapon.

She heard the tiny legs clicking over the leather console as the centipede paraded to the passenger seat and onto Frank's leg.

"Oh, Jesus," Wanda gasped. "Damn it, Frank, WAKE UP!"

The centipede set its fangs into Frank's flesh and rhythmically bobbed its head as it pumped its venom.

Frank's body quaked with a slight shudder.

The razor-sharp mandibles bit into the open wound on Frank's thigh to create a passage for the centipede to enter.

Overcoming her fear, Wanda reached down and grabbed the centipede. She yanked it back in an attempt to extract it out of Frank.

The creature persisted and squirmed to pull free from her grip.

She couldn't believe its powerful strength as it wiggled in her hand and did a half roll onto its arching back. It was like arm wrestling an alien from another planet. The rear section of the centipede rose. Parallel rows of claw-tipped legs clung and pierced her arm like a maniacal sleeve of knives in a torture chamber.

Frank moaned as the centipede gnawed into his leg.

Wanda knew, once the centipede had finished with Frank, she would be next.

Feeling as though she might pass out, she let her head slump on her chest.

And that's when she eyed the tip sticking out of her breast pocket.

With all her resolve, she raised her right arm and snatched the ballpoint pen.

Wanda clicked the end cap, pushing out the pointy end. She came down and stabbed the centipede in the belly. Then she dragged the pen, creating a long slash. An emerald fluid streamed out of the fissure.

The centipede pulled its head out from Frank's thigh to see what was ravaging its body.

But by then, Wanda had done her worst. She felt the grip of the creature's legs weaken. Finally, the centipede let go of her arm and draped over the console.

She closed her eyes and slipped into unconsciousness.

* * *

Wearing a hospital robe and slippers, and her left arm in a sling, Wanda shuffled down the hospital corridor. She entered a room and plopped down on the chair next to the bed.

Frank gazed over and smiled. His head was elevated, as well as his leg. Drainage tubes attached to his open wound fed a yellowish fluid into a clear pouch affixed to the bottom of the side railing.

"How's the leg?"

"Numb, even though I can wiggle my toes." He studied the purplish bruise on the left side of Wanda's face. "Nice shiner."

"Thanks."

"You give that deputy of yours a raise?"

"Oh, I intend to. If he hadn't started a search, we might not have been so lucky."

Deputy Monroe stood in the doorway and knocked on the doorjamb.

"Hi, Arness, we were just talking about you," Wanda said.

"I got some bad news, Sheriff."

"What's that?"

"Last night, some folks were attacked out at the campgrounds."

"Was anyone hurt?"

"Four campers were killed. Ranger Dave Morley's dead, too."

"Oh my God."

Frank shifted in the bed to reposition himself, wincing when he moved his injured leg. "Were there any witnesses?"

"No. The victims were all bit up. Some of them eaten like they were ravaged by wild animals."

Frank and Wanda exchanged knowing looks.

"I got booted out of the campground by the Feds. Said they were taking over."

"It is a national park," Wanda said. She looked at Frank. "They'll probably want our statement."

"Then they'll just have to come and find us. I don't think I'm going anywhere at the moment."

"I'm going back to the office," Deputy Monroe said.

"Thanks for holding down the fort."

"No problem, Sheriff. You just get better."

After the deputy had left the room and was far enough down the hall, Wanda looked over at Frank and said, "Where do you think they went? Surely, they didn't just crawl under a rock and hide."

"They do like dark places."

A food service worker came into the room. The young woman put a breakfast tray on the adjustable bed table. She lifted the cover off the plate and saw Frank's indifferent reaction to the entree.

"It's actually quite good," the woman said defensively.

"Oh, believe me," Wanda told her, "he's eaten worse."

CHAPTER SIXTEEN

Derek leaned the shovel against the tree trunk. He put his arm around Tammy's shoulder and gave her a hug as they stared down at the small mound of earth adorned with pet toys and picked flowers, next to the vegetable garden.

It was windy but a mild sunny day.

"If he hadn't showed up when he did…" Tammy trailed off when the tears came.

"We're going to miss you, little buddy," Derek said in a choked voice.

They stood over Toby's backyard gravesite and cried.

Tammy sat down on the grass. "I think I want to stay here for a while."

"Sure. I'll go unpack the car." Derek walked across the lawn to the detached garage and entered through the side door.

Tammy thought back on all her fond memories of Toby. The time they rescued him from the pound. His antics, the devilish things he'd do getting into trouble but always being forgiven no matter the extent of the damage. She picked up the yellow rubber squeak toy, Ducky, one of Toby's favorites, whenever he was in the tub getting a much-needed bath. Toby had nibbled off the beak.

She had no idea how long she had been sitting there reminiscing. The late-morning sun had shifted, and Tammy was no longer under the shade of the tree. It was getting hot, so she got up and walked over to the side door to the garage.

"Derek?"

She peered inside the gloomy structure. The ice chest and camp stove were on the floor by the rear tire of the car. Some boxes were haphazardly stacked nearby.

Derek was bent over the rear bumper, his upper torso inside the open trunk.

"Honey?"

Something serpentine rippled under the back of his shirt.

She could hear scratching behind the spare tire.

A gust of wind caught the garage side door and slammed it shut.

And that's when Tammy saw them and screamed.

CHAPTER SEVENTEEN

It was midmorning when Jake unzipped the flap of his tent and squinted at the bright sunlight. He slowly crawled out, nursing a terrible hangover. He glanced over at the lake and saw Craig, naked and dripping wet, standing on a boulder.

"Hey, Carver! Come on in, the water's great!"

"No, thanks," Jake replied.

"Wake the girls! We can skinny dip!"

"I don't think so."

"Pussy!" Craig dove into the shallow water.

"Is he out of his mind?" Nora said as she poked her head out of the tent.

"Thinks he's in the Polar Bear Club. How do you feel?" Jake asked.

"You mean my head? Like a zombie's been munching on my brain."

"Mine, too. This is going to be one hell of a day."

Craig climbed out of the water and hollered at the top of his lungs like an escapee from a lunatic asylum and jumped back in.

***

After spending most of the day at the Vista Lake campsite, the hikers trudged down the mountain face, stopping halfway when they reached a fork in the trail.

"Nora? Would you mind reaching in my pack and getting my aspirin?" asked Gail.

"Sure," Nora said. She opened a pouch in the back of Gail's pack and took out a small bottle. She took another glance inside the pouch. "You brought your cell phone? I doubt if you'd get any service up here."

"I didn't think it would hurt to bring it along. You never know. Craig, did you remember to charge our phone?"

"Jesus, what is it with you and cell phones? It's like no one can survive these days unless they've got a damn phone plugged to their ear."

"I just asked if you charged it."

"I heard about this nightclub where they made everyone check in their cell phone," Craig said. "Turns out, half the phones were fakes. Just for show, so all those jerks could look important. Do you believe that shit?"

"I don't mean to upset you, Craig," Jake said, "but I better check my PDA, make sure the GPS is still working." Jake took the hand-held device out of a side pocket of his backpack.

He grinned at Craig. "Yep, working like a charm."

CHAPTER EIGHTEEN

"It's going to be dark soon," Jake said. "We're almost to Twin Lakes."

Twenty minutes later, they were standing at the base of a steep one hundred foot granite wall by the two lakes.

Jake gazed up. "We'll camp up there. That way, we'll have a great view of the valley."

Nora faced Craig and Gail. "You guys, it's a little tricky, so just take your time and you'll do fine." She pointed to the foot-wide granite path slanting up the face of the precipice.

"We're going up that?" Gail asked.

"Like I said, it's a little tricky, so be careful."

Jake went up first. The others followed, staying as close to the rock wall as possible to avoid slipping off the ledge.

Halfway up the path, Gail lost her concentration and teetered on the edge, but Nora grabbed her by the strap of her backpack and pulled her to safety. Gail stared down in horror at the fifty-foot drop to the boulders and water below.

"My God, that was close," she said.

"Nice and easy," Nora said. "We're almost there."

They reached the top and found themselves standing on a glacial butte blanketed with snow. Higher up the mountain were snowcapped crags and another summit.

Jake gazed back from where they had come and marveled at the panoramic view of the entire valley. He went over to a nook that was the perfect place to pitch the tent.

Nora spotted a natural depression in a granite step, eroded into the shape of a bathtub with two feet of frigid water. "What do you think, Gail? Dare we?"

"I will if you will," Gail said.

***

Craig sat on a flat rock, watching the sun melting on the horizon.

He glanced over at the women bathing. Gail was naked as she stepped out of the rock-tub. She began to towel herself off.

Craig's eyes shifted to Nora. He watched her like a voyeur as she got out.

Nora shook her hair, and the rest of her pleasantly jiggled. Goose bumps prickled her thighs and her fine rump as she bent over to slip on her panties.

"Some view, eh?" Jake said, coming up on Craig unexpectedly.

"What?" Craig said, nearly jumping out of his skin.

"The sunset."

"Yeah, right," Craig said, turning his head to look back over the valley.

***

Jake dozed in his sleeping bag outside the dome tent, while Craig slept inside.

Gail and Nora were inside the other tent, tucked in their sleeping bags, but having trouble falling asleep.

"Ever watch CSI Miami?" Gail asked.

"Not that much. I prefer the one with William Petersen. Why?"

"What's Caruso's job?"

"Isn't he the one in charge?"

"I guess. But he never seems to do much, just barks out orders. And watches everyone else work."

"He does shoot the bad guys," Nora said.

"Well, yeah, he does do that."

"Horatio's kind of a cool name."

"I don't know. Sounds like a restaurant."

"You're thinking of The Horn Blower."

"I mean, really, the guy is whiter than white," Gail said. "It's Miami, for crying out loud."

"So he uses a lot of sun block." Nora stretched out a yawn.

"Ever see the way he stands."

"You mean the stiff neck?"

"And those long montages. I swear, each episode they must play an entire album of songs."

"Less script to write."

"I don't get it," Gail said. "Rockford and Columbo never had all that DNA nonsense, and they still solved their cases. Whatever happened to the good old gumshoes?"

"Cable TV teleported them into the land of the reruns. We should try and get some sleep."

"Though, I have to admit, I did like him NYPD Blue."

"Good night," Nora said.

"You think it's true?" Gail asked.

"Is what true?"

"That love conquers all."

"I suppose."

"I could sure use a little bit of love right about now."

"Things will get better, with Craig I mean, you'll see."

CHAPTER NINETEEN

Jake was boiling water for instant coffee when Nora and Gail crawled out of the tent.

"How'd you sleep?"

"Like I do after a night on your mother's pullout couch whenever we visit," Nora said, bending backward to relieve her stiff back.

"Hmm, that bad, huh? How about you, Gail?"

"About the same."

Jake lifted the pan and poured the steaming water into three tin cups. He emptied a packet of Folgers instant coffee into each one and stirred them with a spoon.

"Here, maybe this will brighten your day."

"Smells good," Gail said, as Jake handed her a cup.

"Come check out the view," Jake said to Nora. They carried their coffees over to the edge of the summit and gazed out over the rocky landscape and the nearby forest below. The rising sun was casting a salmon-colored hue over the granite.

"I should take a picture." Jake put his cup down on a flat rock and was about to go get his camera when Gail screamed.

"What the hell?"

Gail had dropped her coffee tin and was flat on her back. A bug-like creature had her pinned to the ground with its long body. Scores of sharp pointy legs were tearing at her clothes. Its head was flush with Gail's and the thing was eating her face.

Jake ran up and grabbed the giant insect. He tried to lift it off of Gail, but it wouldn't let go and only clung tighter. "I need my knife out of my pack," he yelled.

Nora dashed over to Jake's backpack.

Craig lurched out of the tent. "What's going on?" And then he saw the thing attacking his wife. He reached back into the tent and came out with his .45-caliber Colt. He held the big gun in both hands and aimed at the creature gnawing at Gail's face. She kept screaming, especially when the thing ripped out a chunk of her cheek.

"Craig, put the gun down. You'll hit Gail."

Nora found the knife and called out, "Jake!" She threw the knife, almost striking Craig before it landed blade first into the dirt a couple feet from where Jake stood.

Jake pulled the knife out of the ground. He reached down and stabbed the tail end of the creature, cutting off four of its legs.

"What the hell is that thing?" Craig yelled.

"It's a giant centipede," Jake said.

Green blood leaked out all over Gail's jeans. The creature disengaged itself and headed for the nearest rocks.

Craig fired the Colt, but the bullet missed. He shot again only to kick up more dirt.

The centipede scurried away and disappeared into the rocks.

Nora knelt beside Gail, who was already catatonic. The woman could only stare up at them. Half of her face had been savagely gnawed off, her tongue and teeth visible in the gaping hole in her cheek.

"Gail!" Jake reached down and shook her, but she didn't move. "Christ, she's paralyzed."

"Jake, what are we going to do?"

Gail's skin was quickly changing from a normal flesh tone to a bluish shade.

The woman opened her mouth and gasped.

"She's going into anaphylactic shock."

Nora bent down to give Gail mouth-to-mouth.

Jake pulled Nora back. "No, it's too risky. The thing was poisonous."

"We can't just let her die."

"Why not," Craig said. "She's already dead. The cancer was going to kill her anyway."

Jake jumped up and punched Craig in the jaw. The man fell back and went down on one knee.

"What the hell, Craig? She's your wife."

"Don't you ever…" Craig slowly got back on his feet.

"You're nothing but a callous bastard, you asshole," Jake shouted.

Craig raised the gun and fired at Jake. The bullet whizzed by his head.

"Craig, are you out of your mind?" Nora screamed.

Jake dove at Craig and they tussled on the ground. Jake swung with his knife hand to swat the gun out of Craig's hand.

The sharp blade came down and cut through Craig's gun hand, slicing off his trigger finger at the second knuckle and severing his other three fingers.

Craig bawled and dropped the gun. He grabbed his injured hand. Blood gushed out of the wound, splattering the ground and the detached digits.

"Oh my God, Craig. I didn't mean that to happen," Jake said, shocked that he had maimed the man.

"He needs a tourniquet," Nora said but didn't move.

Craig grimaced and groaned, "You're the asshole."

"Okay, Craig, I'm the asshole." Jake looked over at Nora. "We really have to stop the bleeding."

Nora rushed over to the nearest backpack.

While Jake was watching Nora, Craig tucked his bleeding hand under his armpit and picked up the gun.

Jake turned and looked down when Gail let out a strangled wheeze. Her eyes went white as they rolled back in the sockets.

There was a loud boom and Jake fell back. He crashed to the ground. A red splotch blossomed on the front of his shirt.

Nora came running. "Craig, what the hell did you do?" She dropped to her knees and stared down at Jake. His eyes were closed and his breathing was shallow. His shirt was soaked with blood.

Nora stood and glared at Craig. "Have you completely lost your mind?"

"That's what he gets for calling me an asshole."

"Go to hell. Asshole!"

Craig pointed the gun at Nora.

She took a step back and heard a crunch. She looked down and realized that she was on a patch of snow.

Blood was dripping down the side of Craig's shirt from his ruined hand tucked under his armpit.

"I hope you bleed to death."

Suddenly, Nora sunk into the snow up to her waist. It was though she had stepped in quicksand. She put her hands flat on the ground and tried to push up but she was wedged in. Panic swept over her face.

"Oops. Looks like you got yourself in a little situation. Maybe you would like a hand." Craig walked over. "Or should I say a foot." He raised his leg and placed his boot on Nora's shoulder and shoved her down the hole.

She plummeted thirty feet down a deep shaft, and landed hard on the shale bottom of the pit. Pain immediately shot up her left leg.

She looked up.

Craig leaned over the rim and looked down briefly then ducked away.

Nora stared up at the round patch of blue sky. "Craig, come back. You can't leave me down here."

"Who says?"

Nora heard a flapping sound. Then Craig draped a blue tarp over the hole.

"Don't do this!"

The shaft gradually darkened as Craig covered the tarp with snow.

And then it was pitch black.

CHAPTER TWENTY

A nurse pushed Frank out the main doors of the small hospital, which wasn't more than a clinic, as it only had ten beds. Wanda walked behind, carrying a pair of crutches, and followed them to the parking area.

"There you are, Mr. Travis," the nurse said, parking the wheelchair near the curb.

"Thanks for the ride," Frank said, as the woman turned to go back inside the building.

"They must keep her pretty busy. She's the only nurse I saw working."

"That's the way it is in a small town," Wanda said. "Everyone wears multiple hats. She's also the pharmacist."

"You're kidding."

"The hospital administrator is also the X-ray, and the lab technician."

"Sound like hard workers."

"Folks around here do their share."

"How's the arm?" Frank asked.

"I'm hoping after today to lose the sling."

They heard the sound of engines approaching as two cars drove up to the curb.

The first one was a '56 Chevy. The vehicle was in stages of restoration. The body was being prepped for a proper painting as it was covered in gray primer. The right front fender had been patched with Bondo paint filler and was still in need of sanding. All four tires looked fairly new with chrome wheels and baby moon rim hubcaps.

Ryan was behind the wheel. He revved the engine once then turned it off.

"My son just finished rebuilding the engine. She might not be much to look at, but she runs like a top," Wanda said, proudly.

"I had one just like it when I was his age," Frank replied.

Ally climbed out of the driver's side of Ryan's '71 Pontiac Firebird Trans Am. She pulled the seat forward. Dillon jumped out and ran up on the sidewalk.

"Don't think I'm going to pick you up," Wanda said, directing his attention to her sling.

"Jeez, Mom, what happened? Did one of the bad guys wing yah?"

"You might say that."

Ryan got out of the Chevy and walked around. He opened the front passenger door.

Wanda's children looked at Frank.

"Ryan, Ally, Dillon. I want you to meet Frank Travis."

Everyone smiled and shook hands, even Dillon.

"Frank will be staying with us until his leg heals. As he is going to have trouble getting around, I think we should set him up in Dilly's room."

"Where're am I going to sleep?" Dillon asked.

"You can bunk with your brother."

"What?" Ryan said.

"It won't kill you."

"You know, if it's too much of an inconvenience," Frank said.

"Nonsense." Wanda gave Ryan and Dillon a stern look.

"What about Rochelle?" Dillon said.

"Oh, come on. Not her, too." Ryan threw up his hands.

"I'm sure Frank won't mind sharing a room with Rochelle," Wanda said. "Besides, I don't like her going up those stairs. She's not really built for it."

"Who's Rochelle?" Frank asked, wondering what all the fuss was about.

"That's my dog. You're going to love her. She sleeps with me," Dillon said with a big fat grin.

CHAPTER TWENTY-ONE

"So this is what they call a one-horse town," Frank said.

"Not even. Prospect isn't even on most maps. Try looking us up on MapQuest."

Wanda had parked the Chevy in front of the feed store, which was next to the Arco gas station.

A green sign with the name Blackstone Feed Store was mounted over the walk-in entryway that led into a barn-like structure. The front of the building was a facade of upright cedar slats, the wood so aged that most of it was streaked white. Hay bales were stacked under an overhang to keep them out of the elements but also to dress up the place and give it some charm.

The Arco station had a single island with two pumps: one gasoline, the other with diesel. The building had a small front office for coming inside to pay for gas or set up appointments for automobile repair in the single bay garage.

Across the street was Wanda's sheriff office, the Log Jam Diner, and customer parking shared by a small grocery store. Next to the market was a tiny post office, the official USPS logo taking up most of the window next to the entry door.

Farther down was the Crossroads Bar and Lounge, a seedy watering hole frequented by the local barflies and the occasional congregation of bikers passing through.

A bait and tackle shop was next door, along with a beauty salon.

A traffic light was suspended high over the middle of the road by a strung cable even though it wasn't a proper intersection as there was only one side road, and that turned into a dead-end after a quarter-mile stretch into the woods.

"Where are all the homes?"

"Scattered all over. Did you know I used to work out of my house?"

"Really."

"Didn't get a proper place of business until the realtor dropped his lease and moved away. Now it's officially the sheriff's office."

"I guess you're not on much of a budget."

"Not much is right. I need to check up on a couple things before we go to the house. You want to come along or wait here?"

"I think I'll rest the leg. You go on ahead."

Wanda got out of the car and thought she would check with Dale Watson over at the Arco station first. She walked into the bay and found the owner working under the hood of an old Ford truck.

"Hi, Dale."

The man raised his head and smiled. "Hi, yourself, Sheriff. What can I do for you?" He grabbed a shop rag and wiped the grease off his hands.

"You have my Jeep out back."

"Well, no. It was totaled. It got hauled off to the compactor."

"What?"

"After your accident, I thought I'd help you out. Found your information in the glove box and called the insurance company myself. Fella came out, took pictures, and gave me a form for you to sign." The mechanic stepped over to a clipboard hanging on the wall next to the fan belts and pulled off the insurance forms. He came back and gave the papers to Wanda.

"Dale, I wish you hadn't done that."

"Sorry, Sheriff. Thought I'd save you the hassle."

"Well, you were only doing what you thought best. Guess there's not much we can do about it now. Well, you take care then."

"Sorry about the mix up."

Wanda left the filling station. She went over to the feed store and went in through the large entry with an aluminum rollup door housed overhead.

The store was nothing more than a large warehouse. The owners' house was flush against the rear of the building, which made it convenient while running their business during normal operating hours. Sometimes when the store was closed, it made it easier to open up briefly for a farmer or rancher that suddenly needed to restock on feed.

Stacks of various brands of feed for different farm animals were lined up around the establishment. There was a small section for domestic pets.

Wanda went over and checked the limited inventory but didn't find what she was looking for.

"Well, hi there, Wanda," Maxine Blackstone greeted as she came in from the back. She was in her sixties, thin built, but was a vital woman. She carried a twenty-pound bag of chicken feed under one arm and placed it on the counter.

"Maxine. I was wondering if Harmon ordered that special food I asked for. It's the only thing I can get those finicky dogs of mine to eat."

"Let's ask him." She turned and called out, "Harmon! You got a customer!"

Harmon strolled in. A worried look came over his face as soon as he saw Wanda.

"Oh, you're not going to arrest me, are you?"

"And why would I want to do that?"

Harmon was a big man. He took off his gloves and worried them in his beefy hands. "For messing up your order."

"Harmon, I'm just about out. Another day, and I'm going to have to serve up supper for Winston and Rochelle at the dinner table."

"Yeah, you would do that," Harmon laughed. "It'll be here tomorrow. I promise."

"I'm holding you to it. Bye now," Wanda said and gave the Blackstones a friendly wave over her shoulder as she went out the door.

She was almost to the Chevy when a Jeep mail truck pulled up and stopped.

"You know, you could save me a trip out to your place," Jackson Tucker said.

Wanda walked up to the mail truck. The driver's door was slid back.

The town's postal carrier rifled through a stack of mail in his hand. He was a mousy-looking man with a beak nose and a drawn face. He wore thick-lens glasses. Some said he was blind as a bat without them. And being the mail carrier, he knew everyone's business.

"So what do you have for me?"

Jackson sifted through each piece of mail.

"Well, let me see. Here's a *Car and Driver* magazine for Ryan, a letter from one of Ally's friends. Oh, and your gas and electric bill. I got a ton of coupon fliers for the grocery store if you want some."

"No thanks."

"Here's another bill; maybe a license summons for one of your dogs."

"That all?"

"I believe so." Jackson handed Wanda her mail.

She thanked him and walked over to the Chevy.

"Did you get it all done?" Frank asked, once Wanda was back in the car.

"Are you from around here?"

"Why, do I sound like it?" he said.

"Maybe."

Frank made a face and rubbed his leg.

"Is it bothering you?"

"A little."

"Let's go home."

"Sounds good." Frank leaned back in the seat but still managed a smile.

***

Craig emptied Jake's backpack and found a first aid kit. He flipped the lid open with his good hand. He took the small plastic bottle of disinfectant, twisted the cap off with his teeth, and poured the contents over his mutilated hand.

The pain was intense enough to make him scream.

He dug through the bag and pulled out one of Jake's shirts. He ripped the garment down the center and began wrapping his hand.

Craig looked back inside the backpack. He found a roll of duct tape. Getting a corner up with his fingernail, he grabbed the tape in his teeth and peeled back about six inches. He stuck the sticky tape on the makeshift dressing and began wrapping the adhesive around his bandaged hand.

He popped the top off an aspirin bottle and crammed six pills into his mouth and dry-swallowed them.

Craig dumped the rest of the contents out of Jake's backpack. He rummaged through everything, taking only food that he could readily consume without having to cook, and a canteen of water. He found Jake's car keys and put them in his pocket. He went through Nora's pack but didn't find anything worth taking.

He glanced over at Jake, lying on the ground.

Craig sauntered over to the still body, carrying Nora's pack by the strap. He looked down and threw Nora's pack on Jake's chest.

He walked over to Gail. It was difficult to even imagine that mangled face had ever been his wife. He should have felt some remorse, but instead, he was numb inside. He hadn't cared. If anything, he was relieved. The thought of having to play nursemaid to his wife and wait on her hand and foot while she whiled away in her deathbed was too much for him to have to endure. It didn't seem fair that he should have to make such a sacrifice when he could be out having the time of his life.

She was too hideous to look at so he turned away.

He delved through the other backpacks. He took Gail's cell phone and tucked it in his pocket. He'd emptied his pack and filled it with the bare essentials, as he wanted to travel light.

He felt lightheaded and took a moment to clear his head. He wondered if he was too woozy to make it back down the mountain. Hell, he wasn't even sure he knew the way. Then he remembered Jake's PDA that had the GPS.

Craig searched through the clothes and camping equipment strewn on the ground and finally found the device. He turned it on. But after a couple minutes of pushing buttons and not understanding what he was doing, he became frustrated and threw the PDA at a boulder, smashing it to smithereens.

"Piece of shit!"

With his gun tucked in his waistband, Craig picked up his backpack and started his long trek, praying that he could find his way off the mountain.

CHAPTER TWENTY-TWO

When they arrived at the farmhouse, there was a black sedan parked in the gravel driveway that stretched around back to the barn.

"Who do you think that is?" Wanda said.

"That's not your car?"

"No."

"It looks official."

Wanda drove the Chevy past the other car and parked by the backdoor. She got out and helped Frank up the steps that led into the mudroom. He had his leg up as he struggled with the crutches. They went inside the screened room. Wanda opened the door leading into the kitchen. She held it open for Frank while he squeezed through the doorway.

A man in a black suit was sitting at the kitchen table.

Frank nodded and hopped over to a chair and plopped down. He leaned the crutches on the back of the chair.

Ally stepped into the kitchen. "This man is from the FBI, so I let him in to wait for you."

"That's fine, honey," Wanda said.

"I'm going up to my room."

"Okay. Where're Ryan and Dillon?"

"Ryan's out. Dillon is playing in his room with Rochelle."

"Dinner should be ready in an hour."

Ally walked out of the kitchen.

Wanda turned and looked at the man seated at the table. "You're with the FBI?"

"That's right. I'm Special Agent Clint Grover. If you don't mind, I would like to ask you some questions."

"We were expecting you. I suppose you know who I am."

The agent nodded. "And who is this?"

"I'm Frank Travis."

"Mr. Travis." Agent Grover looked over at Wanda. "Do either of you know what happened at the campground?"

"We believe those people were killed by giant centipedes."

"Giant what?"

"Centipedes," Frank said.

"Are you trying to be funny?"

"Not at all," Wanda assured the man.

"I've never heard of giant centipedes in this part of the country."

"That's because they're not indigenous to this region. This particular species originated in the Amazon."

"The Amazon? So how did they end up here?"

"A plane crashed a few days ago. They were part of the cargo. Now they're loose in your national park."

"Do you have proof?"

"I captured one. It's not as big as the giant ones, but at least we can prove that they're here," Frank said.

"Let's take a look."

"Uh, I'm afraid that's not possible," Wanda confessed.

"What do you mean? There's the dead one in your Jeep. And we can show him the live specimen that's in my rucksack," Frank said.

"I'm afraid there was a foul up. The Jeep was taken to the wreckers. It was put in the compactor."

"Well, then. Do you have any other proof?"

"There're carcasses out in the woods."

"How do I know that they weren't killed by some other animal?"

"You don't."

"Well, if that's all you have, I guess I'll be going. If something concrete comes up, give me a call. Here's my card." Agent Grover pulled out a business card and slipped it onto the table.

Wanda walked the agent out. She watched as he got into his car and backed out of the driveway.

Ryan was just arriving in the Trans Am. He let the other car pass before pulling in. He jumped out of his car and trotted up the steps to the front porch.

"Dinner will be along soon," Wanda told her son.

"Great, I'm starved," Ryan said.

They went into the kitchen.

"Hey, Ryan," Frank greeted.

"Mr. Travis."

"Call me Frank. I hate all that formal stuff."

"Okay."

"Oh Mom, I forgot to tell you. I was there when they pulled your Jeep out of the ravine. The guy was nice enough to let me grab all your guys' stuff before he towed it over to Dale's."

"Ryan, you're a lifesaver," Wanda said.

"You got my rucksack?"

"Yeah."

Wanda came over and kissed her son on the forehead.

"Mom? What's going on?"

"Now we can show Grover the specimen you caught," Wanda said to Frank.

"What are you guys talking about?" Ryan asked, befuddled.

"We'll explain in a minute," Frank said. "Where'd you put my rucksack?"

"It's in Dillon's room."

CHAPTER TWENTY-THREE

Dillon sat at his tiny desk, drawing a sea monster. He liked the way he did the head, but the body looked kind of weird. Rather than erase it and try again, he crumpled the paper up and tossed it on the floor where there were twenty other wadded up drawings.

Rochelle lay by his feet. She was gnawing on a rawhide bone. The ends looked like white mush.

Her ears perked when she heard a sound. It was coming from the corner of the room.

Emanating from within Frank's rucksack on the floor.

The bulldog ignored her chewy and got up.

Dillon noticed his dog ambling off.

"Where're you going?"

Rochelle padded up to the rucksack and sniffed the canvas.

She stiffened her shoulders and growled.

"What's wrong, girl?"

The dog pawed at the bag.

Dillon scooted off his chair and crossed the room. "Is it food?" He hadn't eaten much for lunch and had regretted not finishing his sandwich. Dinner wasn't for a while and he was pretty hungry. What if there was a tasty treat inside? He knew he wasn't supposed to get into other people's stuff but maybe there was enough of a snack that if he took just a little, Mr. Travis wouldn't even miss it.

He knelt on the floor and looked at the bag that belonged to their new houseguest.

Rochelle started to whine and pawed at the canvas again.

"What is it, girl?" Dillon reached over and untied the top flap. He looked in and saw the long tube. He reached in and took the cylinder out.

Something was inside. Something alive. He tried peeking through the air holes but couldn't quite see what it was.

He grabbed the twist-off cap in his little hand and turned. At first, it seemed like it was stuck. So he tried again. This time, the cap spun. He continued to unscrew the cap until it had completely come off the last spiraled thread.

His bedroom door suddenly flew open.

It was his mom and Mr. Travis.

They both looked down in horror and yelled, "DON'T OPEN THAT!"

A huge bug raced out of the tube, scaring Dillon and making him scream.

Rochelle drew back, but when she saw that Dillon might be in danger, she sprung into action and ran after the creature that had disappeared under the bed.

"Dillon, get out of there," Wanda ordered her son. Dillon did what he was told and ran as fast as his little legs could carry him out into the living room. Rochelle raced after him.

"We have to get it out from under there," Frank said, leaning on his crutches. "Sorry, but I won't be much help with this leg."

Wanda went to enter the bedroom then stepped back. She turned her head and yelled, "Ryan, get down here. Now!"

He rushed down the stairs, two steps at a time.

"What is it? Is the house on fire?"

"There's a big bug under Dillon's bed."

"Not another tarantula."

"No, honey. It's a centipede."

"Really, you're afraid of a little centipede."

"No, and don't be a wiseass. This thing is deadly."

"Jeez, you don't have to get testy."

Frank looked at Ryan. "Son, your mother's serious. This creature is dangerous."

Ryan could tell by Frank's stern expression that he wasn't kidding. The teenager sped over to the fireplace and grabbed the poker out of the tool stand.

"Good thinking. Maybe you can flush it out with that."

Before Ryan could step into the room, Winston bolted past him.

"Winston, get out of there."

But the dog wasn't listening. It sensed that there was something lurking under the bed, threatening the family, and stuck its nose under the bed frame to sniff it out.

Ryan grabbed Winston's collar and pulled him back just as the centipede charged out from under the bed.

Wanda went to stomp on it as it sped across the threshold, but it was too fast and escaped getting crushed under her boot.

Ally came down the stairs. She had been listening to her music and was taking the earbuds out of her ears when she saw the giant centipede dart across the throw rug and scamper under the china hutch where Wanda kept all of her fine plates and crystal serving dishes for special holidays.

"It went under there!" Ally pointed and jumped up on the couch. "What is that thing?"

Ryan rushed over and swept the poker back and forth between the lower legs of the hutch. The centipede evaded every thrust of the tool.

"Mom, help me pull the hutch away from the wall."

"You can't. It's screwed in."

Ryan looked behind the hutch. "That's okay, I can break the bracket." He shoved the poker against the mounting bracket to shear it off. But it wasn't as easy as he thought. He put his shoulder into it and pried the bracket.

Suddenly, the bracket snapped but Ryan had put too much leverage into it and the hutch teetered away from the wall.

"Look out," Ally shouted as the hutch came down. Everyone jumped back.

"Oh my God," Wanda said as she watched her precious piece of furniture—the dishes and crystal handed down to her from her mother—crash to the floor in a loud explosion of smashing glass and cracking wood.

"It's heading for the kitchen," Ally yelled.

Winston took off after the giant centipede. The bull terrier darted under the kitchen table where the creature was scurrying under a chair to escape. Winston knocked the chair aside and pounced on the thing, snatching the rear part of the body in his teeth and shaking it like a rag doll.

The centipede coiled under Winston's belly and clamped onto the inside of the dog's rear leg with its sharp pointy feet. It extended its forcipules and injected venom into the canine's flesh with its lethal fangs.

Winston let out a startled yelp.

Ryan ran into the kitchen.

Sensing the vibration of approaching danger, the centipede disengaged itself from the bull terrier and slithered across the linoleum floor straight for the back door.

"I don't believe it," Ryan yelled to the others. "It went out through the doggy door."

He looked down at Winston.

The dog was limping, favoring its back leg. He took a couple steps then fell over onto his side.

"Winston's been bit."

Wanda came into the kitchen and knelt down beside Winston. Frank was right behind, standing with his crutches.

"Is he going to die?" Wanda asked, looking up at Frank.

"Not if we act fast." Frank turned and called out, "Ally, bring me my pack."

Ally didn't ask any questions and darted into Dillon's room. She ran back with the rucksack and handed it to Frank.

"Thanks." Frank leaned the crutches against the wall and slowly crouched on one knee. He opened the flap and began rummaging through his bag.

"Found it." Frank pulled both ends of the snakebite kit apart, each one a suction cup. Inside were a scalpel, a lymph constrictor, and an antiseptic swab.

"Hold him down and raise his back leg so I can treat the wound. We need to draw the poison out."

Ryan held Winston down and raised his leg while Wanda consoled her pet.

"He might fight you, but it has to be done," Frank said.

"He's pretty strong," Ryan admitted.

"It's important you hold him down."

"Okay."

"Winston, be a good boy," Wanda said in a calming voice, stroking the back of his ear.

The bull terrier relaxed his muscles.

Ally, Dillon, and Rochelle stood by and watched with concern.

Frank looked at the punctures. The holes were oozing tiny amounts of blood and the pink skin was already reddening with inflammation. He took the scalpel and made a small slit across one puncture then made another small slice forming an X.

Winston whined a little but didn't flinch.

"Good boy, Winston," Wanda said, praising her brave boy.

Frank crisscrossed the other puncture. He took a suction cup and placed it over a puncture and began to squeeze the rubber. "This should pull the venom out of the wound." He kept it up until he was satisfied that he had sucked out the venom then did the same procedure with the other puncture.

He wiped the area with the antiseptic swab.

"Should we rush him to the vet?" Wanda asked.

"Right now, he just needs to rest. I'm sure he'll be fine."

Winston let out a whimper.

Wanda turned her head and looked at the destroyed hutch in the middle of her living room. She suddenly became overwhelmed with despair, seeing her treasured keepsake, ruined, and Winston lying in pain.

It had been a while since she'd had a good cry.

CHAPTER TWENTY- FOUR

Wanda and Frank had been on Highway 50 for the better part of two hours when their turnoff came up. Wanda steered the Chevy onto the off ramp. She had memorized the route from her conversation with Barry Hinderman who had given her directions over the phone.

It had taken some wangling, but Wanda had been persistent, and after some lengthy persuasion, Hinderman finally agreed that they could come to the temporary site that was being used for the National Transportation Safety Board investigation. He told her that plans were being arranged to later transport the wreckage to a proper government facility.

They drove down a long road with only fields on either side.

"That must be it up ahead," Frank said.

The two-story office building was faced with black panels and windows and at first glance resembled a crossword puzzle. Wanda turned into the small parking lot where there were only a few cars. She parked in front of a pole that had a sign that stated that the stall was for Visiting Parking.

Wanda climbed out of the car and waited for Frank to get out.

"Lock it, will you?"

Frank looked over the roof. "Can't you do it?" And then he realized how stupid he'd been. "Oh, yeah. This is a '56 Chevy. No automatic door locks."

"Duh."

Frank pushed the lock button down and shut the door.

"Thank you," Wanda said sweetly, and closed her door.

They stepped up onto the sidewalk and followed it to the front entrance. Frank was walking better and had lost the crutches, even though he did have a slight limp.

Sliding glass doors opened and they found themselves in a small lobby. A security guard in a tan uniform was sitting at a desk, reading a magazine. As soon as he heard footsteps, he shoved his reading material out of sight in an opened drawer and slid it closed.

"Yes, how may I help you?" he asked.

"I'm Sheriff Wanda Rafferty." Wanda motioned with a nod of her head and said, "This is Frank Travis. We have an appointment to see Barry Hinderman."

The security guard looked down at a clipboard on his desk and studied it for a moment.

Wanda glanced around and didn't see anyone else. She wondered how many visitors came to this remote location, if any. Frank and she were probably the first visitors he'd seen in a long while. He was either being thorough or taking his sweet old time in a feeble attempt at making his job seem more important than it really was.

"Oh, yes. Here you are." The security guard looked up and smiled. "Just take the elevator. Second floor. Suite two-oh-three."

"Thanks," Wanda said.

They walked over to the elevator door. Frank pushed the button with the plastic arrow pointing up.

"You don't think we'll get lost," Frank said, sarcastically.

"Well, if we do, I'm counting on you to lead us out of here."

"I've had some experience."

There was a loud ding and the elevator doors parted.

"After you," Frank said, with a gracious sweep of his hand.

"Thank you." Wanda stepped into the lift.

Frank entered next. He turned and looked at the polished-aluminum operating panel. It had three buttons: FL 1, FL 2, and EMERG.

"Hmm."

"Just push the damn button."

Frank pushed the FL 2 button. The doors closed and the lift took them up to the second floor. The doors opened, and Wanda and Frank got out.

They turned right and went down the hall.

Wanda glanced through a glass partition and saw half a dozen employees seated at their desks.

They found the door to Suite 203 to be open.

A gangly man in a rumpled suit was sitting on the corner of his desk with his arms crossed, apparently waiting for them.

Wanda knocked on the doorjamb and stepped into the suite, followed by Frank.

"Well, hi there," Barry Hinderman said. "Come in and have a seat."

Wanda and Frank grabbed the two chairs facing the government inspector, as Hinderman remained sitting on his desk.

"You must be Frank Travis," Hinderman said.

"That's right. So you do remember our conversation."

"That I do. At the time you called, we were just starting our investigation, so I wasn't able to divulge any information. I'm sorry, where are my manners?" He slipped off his desk and extended his hand. "Sheriff, please to meet you. You're from Prospect, is that right?"

Wanda shook his hand. "Yes, we're about two hours away, north on Highway 50. Small little town, blink and you'll miss us. Please, call me Wanda."

"Very well." Hinderman then shook Frank's hand. "Pleased to meet you both. Now, let me tell you where we stand. Before I start, could I offer either of you some water? It's cold."

"I'd love some," Wanda said.

"Sure," Frank said.

Hinderman went over to the water cooler dispenser in the corner of the small office and filled two paper cups. He came back and handed one to Wanda then passed the other cup to Frank.

While Wanda and Frank were taking sips of their water, Hinderman walked around his desk and sat in his chair.

"I understand you mentioned that you knew the pilot," Hinderman asked Frank.

"That's right, Raymond Trodderman."

"He was a friend of yours?"

"Yes."

"Does he have any relatives that you know of?"

"I don't believe so. I know his parents have been dead for some time. He was never married. So, he had no children. He never spoke of anyone related. "

"Shame. We're holding the body."

Wanda looked over at Frank. "Would it help if you saw him?"

"I wouldn't," Hinderman said glumly. "His body was pretty mangled in the crash."

"I understand," Frank said.

"My 'Go Team,' that's what we call our specialists, went through the wreckage with a fine-tooth comb, myself being the investigator-in-charge. Which means we performed a methodical review of the power plants such as the engine and various systems and the functionality of the aircraft."

"What was Raymond flying?" Frank asked.

"A C-23 Sherpa. Any idea where he might have obtained such a plane."

"No, but besides being a renowned entomologist, Raymond was probably the best bush pilot alive. I can't tell you how many near scrapes he'd gotten himself out of."

"Well, sadly, he didn't evade this one."

"Do you know what caused the plane to go down?" Wanda asked.

"Well, we can never rule out pilot error, but…"

"But what?" Frank asked.

"Most of what we looked at checked out, but one of our specialist noted in her report that there was a partially clogged fuel line. Now, there are many things that can cause a fuel line blockage, like for instance impurities in cheap aviation fuel. Of course, deteriorating rubber in an old fuel line can break off and plug it up. I've even heard of army ants bunging one up and causing a crash."

"Do you think it was intentional?" Frank asked.

"You mean, do I think someone sabotaged the plane? I can't rule it out. We are still waiting on a few lab results."

"So your investigation is still on-going," Frank said.

"We're almost there."

"What are the chances that I can have Raymond's belongings?" Frank asked.

Hinderman pondered the question. "Well, we've taken an assiduous amount of photographs of every aspect of the wreckage, and of Mr. Trodderman's belongings. Of course, I will have to retain his passport. I'm sure you know that he had a very interesting journal and sketchbook, which we still need to photocopy."

"Well, I know that Raymond was a gifted artist and often drew insects from memory, especially when he hadn't the opportunity to capture them on film."

"Some of the drawings are quite remarkable," Hinderman had to confess. "I was quite impressed. Something you might expect to see in an art gallery."

"What are the chances I could take the journal?" Frank asked.

"Like I said, we still need to have it photocopied."

"And how long would that take?"

"A few days."

"Would it be all right if we borrowed the journal, just for a couple of days?" Wanda said. "I'll take complete responsibility."

"Well, it's highly irregular…"

"Let Frank look at it. Maybe there's something in it that might shed some light on what really happened; something only an entomologist could decipher."

"You know, that might be helpful. Okay, here's what I can do. Fill out some paperwork, and give me your word, that if at any time, I request that you return the journal, you comply right away. Is that agreed?"

"That's more than fair," Frank said.

"I'll make sure nothing happens to it."

"I have full faith in you, Wanda. After we're through here, would you care to take a look at the plane? I was thinking of taking a little stretch anyway. I'm not much of a desk jockey, prefer being out in the field."

"That was going to be my next question," Frank said.

"All right then, I could use some fresh air."

CHAPTER TWENTY-FIVE

After locking the journal in the Chevy's trunk, Wanda and Frank followed Hinderman along the front of the building and around the corner. Near the back was a compound surrounded by a ten-foot-tall cyclone fence topped with coiled razor wire.

Hinderman led the way inside the fenced-in area to three flatbed trailers.

The first trailer was loaded up with the C-23 Sherpa's severed wings, the tail section, and the rear ramp. The parts of the plane were stacked on top of each other and fastened down with heavy-duty straps drawn tight by turnbuckles. The two destroyed Pratt & Whitney turboprops were butted side by side on the front of the trailer.

The crushed cockpit on the twisted fuselage was on the second trailer.

Frank could see Raymond's blood on the cockpit's windshield.

The third trailer had been reserved for what was left of the cargo, which was nothing more than smashed-up crates; some of them piled kindling.

"As you can see, the crash had to have been horrendous," Hinderman said. He held a clipboard in his right hand with a summary report of the NSTB investigation, just in case Frank or Wanda had any questions that he might not know the answer off the top of his head.

Frank walked over to the third trailer, the one with the damaged crates.

"Was there a manifest or flight log?" he asked.

"No, which is a FAA violation."

"So there's no way of knowing where Raymond took off from or where he was really heading?" Wanda asked.

"Which is something drug runners do," Hinderman said.

"Believe me, Raymond was no drug smuggler. Though he was known to indulge in peyote on occasion."

"You don't think…" Wanda wondered aloud.

"We did a toxicology," Hinderman said. "His blood work was clean."

"That's a relief." Frank looked over the ruined crates. "What was the longest crate you found?"

Hinderman glanced down at the report in his hand. "Let's see…" He flipped through a couple pages. "There were two, both in pretty bad shape, probably around twenty-feet long."

"Did you find anything usual in any of the crates?" Frank asked.

"Well, now that you mention it, yes. In the large crates, we found strange spores, like excrement. Big as your fist."

"Do you have any idea what they were from?" Frank asked.

"Still waiting for the lab to get back to us."

"Mind if I take a look inside one?"

"Sure, I'll give you a step up." Hinderman placed the clipboard on the lip of the trailer and laced his fingers together.

Frank held onto the trailer and placed his foot into Hinderman's hands. He went to rise but only got halfway up when he got a sharp pain in his recuperating leg where he had been sutured. He immediately dropped to the ground, almost taking Hinderman down with him.

"Jeez, I'm so sorry. I think I may have popped a stitch."

"Well, we wouldn't want that," Hinderman said. "Is there anything else I can do for you both? I should really be getting back inside."

"No, I think you've been quite helpful," Frank said.

"Don't worry. I'll take good care of the journal," Wanda assured the inspector.

"I trust you will. It was nice meeting you both."

Frank and Wanda shook Hinderman's hand once more.

The three walked around to the front of the building. Frank and Wanda went to the car while Hinderman returned to work.

"Well, looks like that went quite well," Wanda said, pulling out of the visitor space and heading out of the parking lot.

"Exceptionally well, I'd say," Frank replied.

As they got on the road, they passed a gray Dodge Ram parked on the shoulder.

It wasn't until the Chevy was almost out of sight that two heads popped up in the cab of the parked truck. The driver started the engine and drove toward the fenced-in compound next to the two-story building.

***

"Interesting reading?" Hinderman asked the security guard as he strolled into the lobby.

The guard stuffed the magazine back in his drawer. "Not really."

"Must get pretty boring sitting down here all day."

"Hey, these days, a guy's lucky just to have a job."

"Yeah, that's for sure. Well, talk to you later." Hinderman started to head for the elevator when he remembered leaving his clipboard back on the trailer. "Crap."

"What's wrong?" the security guard asked.

"Left something in the compound. I'll be right back."

Hinderman went outside and walked around the front of the building, but when he was almost to the entrance of the compound, he saw two figures skulking by the flatbed trailers.

"Can I help you?" Hinderman boomed in an authoritative voice.

He was taken aback at the sight of the two men as they stepped out from behind the trailers.

One man was wearing a light brown fedora with a water-stained band. He had deeply tanned skin from spending long periods outdoors under the scorching sun. His leather coat was made of cowhide, and his trousers and boots were well worn. He had a holstered gun: a German Luger, the same kind of pistol the Nazis used during the Second World War.

With him, was a small, dark-skinned man that looked like an indigenous tribal Indian that had just stepped out of the jungle. His hair was black, bowl cut, with a mud-caked texture and streaked with wide bands of red. His eyes shone like shiny black marbles. Strange squiggly tattoos covered most of his face. A straw-like stick—or maybe it was a thin bird bone—was pierced through the septum below his nostrils.

He looked as though he was in the early stages of becoming Christianized, wearing a white cotton shirt, a pair of brown cargo shorts, and leather sandals. A pouch hung from his belt loop.

The man wearing the hat spoke, "I am Bron Kepler. I was employed by Professor Trodderman."

"Well, if it's back wages you're seeking, I'm afraid you came to the wrong place," Hinderman said. The Indian smiled at him, which gave him the creeps. "Who's your friend?"

"Hondo? He assists me whenever I feel the need for his services."

"What, like a sidekick?" Hinderman looked at the Indian.

The Indian only smiled.

"Can't he speak English?" Hinderman said, addressing Kepler.

"Hondo doesn't speak. That would require a tongue."

"What?"

"When he was a boy, his village was raided. He witnessed his entire family slaughtered. Then he was forced to watch as they were eaten."

"Eaten?" Hinderman said with shock.

"Yes, by cannibals. When it was Hondo's turn, they started by cutting out his tongue, some kind of ritual. Hondo managed to escape."

"Lucky fellow."

"Five years later, he hunted them down and torched their village while they slept. Those that tried to escape the fire, he killed with his poison darts. He's quite skilled with a blowgun."

"What's with the facial tattoos?"

"His people believe that they ward away evil spirits. Hondo hopes to transform into a predator animal some day. A black leopard."

"How do you communicate if he can't talk?"

"We just do."

"Why are you snooping around?"

"I was assisting Professor Trodderman with his research and believe that he may have taken some of my work with him when he left the Amazon. I had hopes of publishing a scientific paper."

"Well, we did find a large journal complete with drawings and photographs."

"That would be it."

"I'm afraid I gave it to the sheriff that was just here."

"Perhaps I could contact him."

Hinderman smiled. "It's Sheriff Wanda Rafferty."

"Oh. Where might I find this Sheriff Rafferty?"

"In a small town called Prospect. It's a two-hour drive north, on Highway 50."

"Then that's where we'll go."

"You'd be wasting your time. She won't give it to you. It's on loan. I'll need it back for my investigation."

"Well, then, I guess we won't be taking up any more of your time," Kepler said, and the two men walked off.

"Strange birds," Hinderman said and shook his head. He went over to the flatbed trailer, collected his clipboard, then walked back to the lobby.

Hondo paused before getting into the passenger side of the truck when he spotted a large crow in a nearby tree. He reached into his pouch and took out his blowgun. He inserted a long dart with a green-feathered tail into the tube.

He swelled his cheeks, and blew.

A second later, the dart struck the bird in the head.

The Indian caught the crow before it hit the ground. He opened the truck door and climbed in.

Kepler was already sitting behind the steering wheel.

Hondo placed the bird on his lap and yanked out the dart. He opened the flap on his pouch, exposing its contents.

Kepler glanced over and saw the sleeves inside, each with different colored feathered-tailed darts. The green-feathered darts were non-lethal and were used by Hondo to kill small birds and rodents for consumption. Yellow-feathered darts were tipped with fast-acting paralyzing venom. The red-feathered darts were extremely poisonous and had been tipped with toxin extracted from the golden poison frog—a single amphibian potent enough to kill twenty men.

Hondo shoved the green-feathered dart into its proper sleeve and placed his blowgun back inside the pouch.

He began plucking the bird, tossing feathers onto the floor mat.

"Must you?"

Hondo looked over at Kepler and gave him one of his creepy grins. He grabbed the bird's head between his thumb and forefinger, and with one quick twist, he wrenched the head off.

"Do not eat that in here," Kepler said.

The Indian smiled and popped the tiny head into his mouth. He bit down with a loud crunch.

"Savage." Kepler started the engine, put the truck in gear, and drove off down the road.

CHAPTER TWENTY-SIX

Nora had never been so scared in her life. Being engulfed in darkness was terrifying. But then she remembered she was wearing her coat with the electroluminescence material. She activated the panel on her coat sleeve, and the shaft lit up. She could see snowmelt dripping down the tubular walls.

It was like standing in a small closet. She felt around the rock and realized that she was boxed in. She raised her hand. A faint breath of air grazed her palm. She was certain that it was coming from somewhere just above her head.

Nora grabbed a nub of rock and shoved her back against the stone and pushed up, placing one boot above the other on the opposite wall. She'd ascended no more than two feet before the rock became too slick and she fell back down.

She made another attempt, and that too failed.

Again she tried, but it was no use. The rock was too slippery.

She was getting frustrated and needed a distraction, fearing that she might panic.

Then she thought back to when she was a child attending Sunday school.

"How did that prayer go? Oh, yeah. The Lord is my rock."

She reached up with one hand.

"I will call upon the Lord...so shall I be saved from mine enemies..."

Her other hand grabbed the rock.

"The floods of ungodly men made me afraid!"

She lifted her boot and found a foothold.

"In my distress, I called upon the Lord, cried unto my God!"

Her fingertips clung to a slippery jut of stone.

She yelled, "He heard my voice! And my cry came before Him! Even into His ears!"

Nora slipped and slid back down. She bowed her head, but before she could succumb to defeat, she heard muffled sounds above and looked up.

The tarp pulled away and clumps of snow hailed down, conking Nora on the head and shoulders.

Nora studied the silhouette of the man staring down at her.

"Oh, my God!"

CHAPTER TWENTY-SEVEN

Jake opened his eyes and had to squint the sun was so bright. His shoulder was burning like someone had driven a hot poker into his flesh. He was surprised to see the backpack on his chest. When he went to push it off, the pack wouldn't move. It was stuck to his shirt.

He remembered being shot by Craig. The stupid bastard must have put the backpack on him. If only he'd thought more of what he had done, Craig might have thought twice about his action.

The weight and the waterproof fabric had acted as a perfect compress on Jake's wound.

Craig had unknowingly prevented Jake from bleeding to death.

Jake gently tugged at the backpack until it became unstuck. He was worried that the bleeding would resume but was relieved to see that the blood covering the bullet wound had coagulated when he peeked under his shirt.

He rolled to one side and looked at the ground where he had been lying. A patch of dried blood had formed under his shoulder. The bullet had gone completely through. At least he didn't have to worry about the bullet being lodged in his body. Chances of the wound becoming infected were greatly reduced, but he was still in need of immediate medical attention.

Jake struggled to get on his knees. Not wanting to reopen the wound, he slowly rose to his feet.

The campsite looked like it had been hit by a tornado. Clothes were scattered everywhere, along with the camping gear. He counted three backpacks.

He looked around and wondered where Nora was. He prayed that she wasn't with that maniac Craig. If he hurt her, Jake would hunt him down and get great pleasure killing the menace.

Wandering around the campsite, Jake searched for items that he could use. He found his PDA smashed on a rock. Most of the readily edible food was gone. Craig had taken one of the canteens, and drained the others. He searched Gail's backpack. The cell phone was gone.

He found the hatchet lying under a pair of shorts. At least it was something.

His knife was nowhere to be seen. Craig could have taken it with him or tossed it over the edge of the cliff.

He was about to head to the trailhead that led down the escarpment when he thought he heard someone ranting. It was faint, almost like he was in an upstairs apartment and he was overhearing someone downstairs.

"Hey!" he yelled.

He could still hear the muffled voice. He began to walk toward the source of the sound. His boots crunched on a patch of hard-packed snow.

The toe of his right boot kicked up something blue. He knelt and was surprised to see a portion of a tarp hidden under the snow. The voice seemed to be coming from beneath.

Jake pulled back a section of tarp. Sheets of snow slide off and fell into a hole in the rock.

He made sure not to slip in and looked down.

A voice said, "Oh, my God!"

"Nora?"

Nora stared up from the bottom of the shaft. "Jake, I can't believe it. You're alive!"

"That I am. What are you doing down there?"

"I fell it, what do you think?"

"Did Craig have anything to do with it?"

"Yeah. The bastard pushed me in."

"What was all the noise you were making?" Jake asked.

"I was reciting a prayer I remembered as a kid."

"You were pretty loud. I wouldn't be surprised if the Man Himself didn't hear you the way you were yelling."

"Jake, are you going to keep on blabbing or are you going to get me the hell out of here?"

"I don't know. I don't have any rope."

"Did Craig leave anything behind?"

"Some clothes, but I don't think there's enough to tie together that would reach down there."

Nora thought for a moment. "I think there's a side passage above me but I can't reach the lip. It's too slippery down here. Every time I try to climb up, I slide down."

"How high up do you need to get?"

"Maybe four feet. If I can get that high, I'm sure I could pull myself up on the ledge."

"I could throw some rocks down."

"Sure, and kill me."

"I've got a better idea. Hang loose for a few minutes."

"Sure, what else am I going to do?"

Jake stood and walked over to the campsite. He gathered up the loose clothing and stuffed the garments into one backpack. He zipped the bag up and carried it over to the rim of the hole.

"I'm going to drop this backpack down. It's only filled with clothes so it's not too heavy, but you can use it to step on. Turn around and face that way," Jake said, and pointed. "I'll try and aim for this side so it won't hit you. I'd cover your head."

Nora turned and hugged the wall with her body. She draped her right arm over her head. "Okay, I'm ready."

"Bombs away," Jake said and released the strap on the backpack.

The bag full of clothes looked like it was going to fall straight down, but ten feet before hitting the bottom, the pack struck a jutted edge of rock and veered off course, striking Nora in the shoulder.

"Hey!"

"Are you okay?" Jake called down.

"Yeah. You make one hell of a lousy bombardier."

"Sorry. See if that helps out."

Nora shoved the backpack against the wall and stepped on it. She reached up but was still a foot or two shy of reaching the ledge.

"I need something more."

"Okay. Hold on." Jake went back and collected the other two backpacks. He glanced around, but there wasn't anything else for him to put in the packs with the exception of rocks.

He looked down at the white ground. He could use snow. He'd have to work fast before it melted but it just might work. He went back to the hole and gazed down.

"I have an idea. I'm going to use snow. It shouldn't be that heavy, so if you do get hit, it's not going to hurt too bad."

"That's a comfort," Nora said.

"Anyway, once I drop them down, you better work fast before they melt."

"All right."

Jake rushed over and began scooping snow into the backpacks. In his haste, he realized that he had reopened his wound. A light trickle of blood seeped down the front of his shirt.

After stuffing both backpacks with snow, he dragged them over to the hole.

"Okay, here they come." He let go of the first one. It plummeted all the way down and landed a foot away from Nora. The second bag missed her as well.

"Right on target," Nora hollered.

She stacked all three backpacks on top of each other and managed to step up. She grabbed the lip of the ledge and pulled herself up.

There was a narrow fissure, but she thought she could fit through. She stuck her hand in and used her electroluminescent coat sleeve as a flashlight. It was definitely a passage, and it looked big enough for her to crawl inside. She could feel cool air on her face. She looked up at Jake.

"There's a tunnel. I can feel a draft."

"Which means that it should lead to a way out."

"Should I go see?"

"Go ahead. While you're doing that, I'm going to go back down and see if there's a cave entrance or something. We're going to get you out. Don't worry. If I don't find anything, I'll come back. Let's say in about thirty minutes."

"Okay. Jake?"

"What?"

"I love you."

"I love you too, babe."

CHAPTER TWENTY-EIGHT

Frank sat at the Rafferty's kitchen table and had just opened Trodderman's journal when Dillon came in and sat down beside him. The boy had brought along a jar with a spider trapped inside.

"What've you got there?"

"Spider."

"Can I see?"

"Sure." Dillon passed the jar over to Frank.

"Do you know what kind of spider this is?"

"Hmm, no?"

"The scientific name is *Hogna carolinensis*."

"A what?"

"Commonly known as a Carolina wolf spider. It usually hunts at night. Wolf spiders like to lay traps under the dirt." Frank made a quick theatrical move with his hand. "And hop out and grab their prey."

Dillon jumped in his seat.

"Sorry, I didn't mean to scare you."

"You didn't scare me."

"What do you say we set him free, so he can go hunt?"

"Okay."

Frank picked up the jar and rose from the table. He opened the backdoor that led into the mudroom. Dillon followed him. Rochelle who was fast asleep by a row of shoes. She had her head on a pair of Dillon's boots.

They tiptoed by the snoring bulldog.

Frank got down on his knees. He unscrewed the lid on the jar. He reached through the mudroom doggy door and released the spider.

"There."

"Now mister wolf spider can go hunt," Dillon said, seemingly just as proud setting the bug free as he was capturing it.

They went back inside the kitchen.

"You thirsty, Mister Travis?"

"You can call me Frank."

Dillon smiled, liking the idea that he could call a grown up by his first name. In school, he had to address his first-grade teacher as Mrs. Katz or the principal as Mr. Donovan. He doubted they even had first names.

The boy walked over to the refrigerator while Frank sat down at the table.

Dillon opened the fridge door and took out two small bottled waters. He shut the door and carried the waters over to the table.

"Thank you, Dillon."

"You're welcome, Frank."

"So do you know what we have here?"

Dillon looked down at some of Trodderman's sketches.

"Fancy drawings?"

"Yes. Made by a great entomologist." Frank twisted the cap off his bottled water and took a sip.

"What's that?" Dillon asked, taking a drink of his water.

"Someone who studies insects."

"Oh, I want to be a en…ento…ologer."

"It's entomologist, but that's close enough. So what do you know about insects?"

"They bite and make you sick."

"Well, there are those. You should be careful when you're collecting bugs, Dillon. You especially don't want to pick them up with your bare hands. You should always wear gloves. You never know. Get bit by a black widow or a recluse spider and you're right, they'll make you sick."

"I saw a spider in the woods. Looked like a black widow but it didn't have that red on its belly."

"You mean the hourglass."

"That's right."

"That's what's known as a false black widow. They're less harmful to humans, but I'd leave them alone. You know, in different parts of the world, people use insects for medicine."

Dillon's eyes lit up. He'd been giving Frank his utmost attention, which was a rarity as the boy was usually far too fidgety to stay in one place for very long.

"For instance, the venom of a South America devil ant has been used to help patients with arthritis. That's when people get old and their bones start to hurt. In Asia, healers use the extract from silkworms to treat various ailments like heart disease, seizure disorder, even flatulence."

"What's that?"

"You mean flatulence?"

"Yeah, that word."

Frank looked around like he was making sure that there was no one else around then leaned in close and whispered, "Farting."

Dillon broke out laughing.

"It's true, I'm not making it up."

"You're not making what up?" Wanda asked, strolling into the kitchen.

Frank and Dillon exchanged looks then began to laugh.

Wanda looked at Dillon. "Well, laughing boy. I just walked by your room. I think there's a few things that need to go in the toy box."

"Oh, Mom, we were—"

"Dillon! Room first, then you can come back."

"Okay." Dillon climbed down from his chair and left the kitchen.

"So, what was so funny?"

"You know, guy talk. I was explaining how certain insects were used medicinally."

"Really?"

"Yeah, did you know that in China they use the blister beetle to treat erectile dysfunction? They're version of the Spanish fly."

"You don't say. I hope you weren't sharing that with Dillon."

"No," Frank laughed. "Just like I didn't tell him about the black mountain ant, which is said to work better than Viagra."

"Okay, Dr. Kinsey. Have you had a chance to look at the journal?"

"No. Come sit down. I think you'll find Raymond's work quite fascinating."

"Sure. Care for some coffee?"

"Yes, I'd love a cup," Frank said, unsnapping the cover and opening up the leather bound book.

A slapping noise caught his attention and he turned in his seat.

Rochelle had just passed through the doggy door and was heading over to her water dish. She lowered her head and lapped up the water. Once she was done, she moved over to her food dish, which was empty.

Wanda finished pouring the two cups of coffee and brought them over to the table. She looked down at Rochelle who was looking up at her with an expectant expression that translated to: *Well, where's my food?*

Winston sauntered into the kitchen. He was favoring his back leg as he strolled up to his food dish. He licked the empty bowl.

Opening up the pantry door, Wanda reached in and grabbed the dog food bag off the floor. She gave it a shake. A few nuggets rolled around inside the bag.

Wanda divvied equal portions into each bowl, which were really nothing more than treats, and not full meals.

The dogs gobbled up their food in seconds flat.

"Remind me we have to go into town later and pick up their food."

"Sure," Frank said. "I have to say, they're great-looking dogs."

"Well, thank you. We used to have another bulldog, his name was Rocky, but sadly, he died. Dillon was heartbroken, so we got him Rochelle. She's a little sweetheart."

"Winston's a pretty magnificent animal. They both are."

Winston raised his white, egg-shaped head and looked up at Frank with his tiny triangular eyes. At just over forty pounds, Winston was a sturdy, muscular dog.

"I'm just glad they don't have to undergo the same abuse their ancestors had to endure."

"Oh, and what was that?"

"You've heard of bull baiting?"

"That term escapes me," Frank had to admit.

"Well, back in the nineteenth century, bulldogs were pitted up against bulls."

"Hardly seems fair."

"It was a blood sport. A bull would be staked out on a length of rope and then be set upon by a pack of bulldogs. Once one of the dogs fastened its teeth on the bull's snout, it was pretty much over for the bull."

"Sounds barbaric. I can't see Rochelle tangling with a bull."

"She'd probably lick him to death."

"Is Winston any relation to the bulldog?"

"Actually, he is a cross between a terrier and a bulldog. After they outlawed bull baiting, dog fighting became more popular. But they found that the bulldog was too bulky and not as entertaining to watch brawl, so they breed a smaller version, the bull terrier."

"He does look like a scrapper," Frank said.

"Oh, he can take care of himself. But he's a good dog. Living out here, it's good to know when I'm away, he's here looking after the kids. He's my white cavalier. That's what they used to call his breed. Bull terriers never picked fights, they ended them."

Frank looked down at Winston and Rochelle, who were lying down by their empty food dishes. "They're quite the pair."

"Yes, they are," Wanda said, and sat down at the table. "So what do we have here?" she asked, referring to the open journal.

"Pretty much Raymond's lifework: his expeditions and his zoological interpretations. He was a brilliant entomologist." Frank turned a page. Tucked inside were some of Trodderman's sketches, each drawn in exquisite detail and colored in with either pencil or oil paints.

"They look so lifelike," Wanda said.

"I think Raymond was as good as John Audubon when it came to his etchings."

"You know, if I squint my eyes, they actually look like photographs."

"See this one," Frank said, pointing at a white crab-like looking insect. "That's a tongue-eating sea louse."

"Vile little creature."

"It's a parasite. It attaches itself to the tongue of another animal and literally drinks the blood."

"Like a vampire?"

"Oh, far worst. As the tongue withers, the louse increases in size. Soon, it's devoured the tongue completely. The host now has the bloated louse for a tongue."

"That's disgusting. Now you know why I hate bugs."

"I'm not finished. Pretty soon the thirsty bugger drains the animal dry."

"What a strange world."

"Oh, it gets stranger." Frank tapped his finger on another sketch. "That's a mind-control beetle."

"You don't say."

"It's true. It usually bites rodents and lays its eggs under the rats' skin then injects them with toxoplasma venom."

"And what does that do?"

"Well, the infected rats show no fear of predators. Which makes them easy prey for cats. The cats eat the larva-infested rats and become infected as well. Then when the cat defecates, presto, out pops more mind-control beetle larvae."

"But they're not harmful to us, right?"

"I once observed a villager who had been bitten by one. He went absolutely mad."

"Flip the page."

"Sure," Frank said, sensing that Wanda didn't duly share his enthrallment with these macabre insects.

He passed over a few pages and stopped when Wanda touched his hand.

"Those are beautiful."

Frank pulled out some loose pages and arranged them on the table.

They gazed at the array of different patterned butterflies. The colors were stunning.

"Judging by these, Raymond traveled far and wide to find these subjects. Truly amazing." Frank scooped up the pictures and stacked them back in the book. He flipped to the next page.

"Oh my," Wanda said.

They were looking at the most bizarre creatures on the planet: a wasp-like insect with a Mohawk headdress; a brown beetle with a Jimmy Durante nose; a purple horny-toad bug with weird eyes.

"See, insects can have a sense of humor." He turned the page.

Frank studied the picture.

"What's that bug?"

"I have no idea. I've never seen it before." Frank read over some of Trodderman's notes.

"Well?" Wanda asked impatiently.

"This is remarkable. Raymond's actually discovered a species of insect with a protein that has the ability to…" A strange look came over Frank's face.

"To do what?"

"Cure cancer. At least that's what I believe, if I'm reading this right. Even has the GPS location with latitude and longitude where the species can be found. This is incredible."

"Oh my God," Wanda said. "So this is what Trodderman wanted you to see."

The kitchen phone rang.

"Let me get that." Wanda pushed out of her chair and went over to answer the phone cradled on the kitchen counter.

"Hello? Oh, hi. Yes, we're looking at it right now. Really. No, I don't know them. Okay. Thank you for the call. We'll keep in touch. Bye," Wanda said and placed the phone back in the cradle.

"Who was that?" Frank asked, noting the concerned look on Wanda's face.

"That was Barry Hinderman. Seems two men showed up after we had left and were snooping around his compound, checking out the plane wreckage."

"Did he get their names?"

"Well, yes. A Bron Kepler—"

"Bron Kepler!" Frank almost jumped out of his chair.

"What's wrong?"

"Kepler is one murderous thief, that's what. I suppose Hondo was with him."

"Hinderman did make mention of some creepy Indian guy."

"That's Hondo. He's a sociopath. What in God's name are they doing here?"

"Hinderman believes they were looking for Trodderman's journal."

"Makes perfect sense. Kepler must have gotten wind of Raymond's find. If he gets his hands on this journal, you can damn well bet he's going to sell it to some pharmaceutical company or the highest bidder. Put in the wrong hands, they'll either put a drug out on the market that will be outrageously priced, or they'll squelch it altogether, and no one will every know it exists."

"Think he had anything to do with the plane crashing?"

"I'd bet money on it. Kepler's a snake in the grass," Frank said, flipping a page in disgust.

He looked down and stared at a photograph.

"What is it?" Wanda came over and sat in the chair next to Frank. She leaned in for a closer look. "Surely, that can't be real. Tell me that picture hasn't been photoshopped."

"Raymond would never do that."

"Who are those people?"

"Pigmies."

"How tall is a pigmy?"

"Average height, just over four feet tall."

Five pigmy Indians were lying on their backs—head to toe—in a straight line on the ground in the form of a measuring stick.

"What in the world is that thing lying beside them?"

Frank studied a page of Trodderman's notes.

He looked at Wanda with an awestruck expression.

"Raymond calls it *Scolopendra Maximus*."

"Is it dead?"

"Looking at the picture I'd say so. It's belly up."

"You don't think Trodderman had these on his plane?"

"I'm beginning to suspect so, yes."

Frank glanced back at the notations on the page.

"And by Raymond's notes, these things have an incredible reproductive rate."

They looked back at the unbelievable photograph.

The centipede lying next to the pigmies was as long as they were.

Wanda went over and grabbed the phone. She fished in her shirt pocket and pulled out a business card.

"Calling Grover?"

"Maybe he'll believe us when you show him that picture."
She looked at the card and pushed in his number on her phone.

"It's ringing."

"Here, let me listen in," Frank said, and got up from the table.
He put his head next to Wanda's.

"This is Special Agent Clint Grover with the Federal Bureau
of Investigation. I am not available to take your call at the present
time. Please leave your name and number and I will get back to
you as soon as possible."

"Hello, Agent Grover. This is Sheriff Wanda Rafferty. I need
for you to call me immediately. You should have my home phone
number. This is urgent. Frank and I have something you really
need to see. Please call me right away." Wanda ended the call.

"Of all times to get his voicemail," Frank said.

"Just give him time," Wanda said. "He'll call."

***

FBI Special Agent Clint Grover was on a return trip to
Prospect, driving through a remote forest region of the park and
coming around a bend when the four-point buck stepped into the
middle of the road. Grover cut the wheel to the left thinking the
animal would bolt in the direction it was facing, but instead, it
turned around to dart back the way it had come.

Grover cranked the wheel the other way and stood on the
brake pedal. He knew he had over-compensated the moment he
reacted. The sedan swerved and fishtailed toward the shoulder
barrier. Before Grover knew it, the car was smashing through the
guardrail—the airbag exploding in his face—and he was soaring
off a steep cliff.

The car nosed down. The bumper struck an outcrop of rock,
spinning the car over in a tumbling motion. As it plummeted, the
sedan careened off the rocky precipice and crashed into a stand of
scrub oaks surrounded by a thick overgrowth of brush.

When the car landed on its roof, Grover knew he was in big
trouble. He was dangling upside down still strapped in his
shoulder harness and seat belt. His right arm was badly mangled,
as it had shoved through an opening in the steering wheel and
wrenched back, snapping the bone. His left arm was pinned under
the armrest.

The pain coursing through his body was unbearable.

His legs were crushed under the dashboard. He could feel the hot metal of the engine scorching his feet through his patent leather shoes.

His cell phone began to play a Stars Spangled Banner ring tone.

He jerked his head around looking for his phone. Last time he remembered, he had left it on the seat next to him.

Now it was somewhere lost in the wreckage.

The phone kept playing the patriotic theme.

The music stopped as the caller was routed to his voicemail.

Hanging inverted, the blood was rushing to his head. He looked out the driver's window. Most of the safety glass had shattered and fallen out, leaving a gaping hole large enough to push a basketball through. A few branches were protruding into the car.

He could hear something moving about in the bushes.

Then he saw what it was. The thing was unbelievable huge.

It scampered through the hole in the glass, scraping its sides as it entered the car.

Grover now wished he had taken the sheriff more seriously, as maybe he wouldn't be hanging like a slab of meat on a hook being eaten alive.

He didn't even get to scream.

CHAPTER TWENTY-NINE

Nora was able to stand upright for only about twenty feet going into the narrow passage before it began to gradually taper. She stooped her shoulders and kept her head down. She could hear the constant drip from the ice melt on the surface, seeping down within the rock. The passage was slick under her boots, and twice, she almost slipped.

Her ankle would tweak with pain every few steps. It was sprained, but she'd power through it. She was lucky she hadn't broken both her legs falling down the shaft.

She could feel the reassuring draft of cool air on her face. She was so relieved that Jake was okay. Being trapped down here and not knowing what had happened to him would have been too painful to bear. But now that she knew he was up there, and was trying to find a way for them to reunite, it gave her the strength to persevere.

The ceiling slanted downward, making it hard for her to walk, as she had to stoop in an uncomfortable posture. Eventually, the tunnel became so low, she had to get down on her hands and knees.

Something clammy scampered across her left hand.

Nora jerked her hand up.

The cave salamander's tiny shadow was projected on the wall by the electroluminescence glow of her coat sleeve. The amphibian dashed across the granite ground and disappeared into a crack in the rock.

Nora took a deep breath.

She could taste the crisp, clean mountain air; like when they'd stopped at that flowing stream and dipped their Sierra cups. The water had been so refreshing. Just thinking about it made her thirsty. Maybe she would come across an underground aquifer, which seemed likely with all the seepage leaking down from the surface.

Nora continued to crawl on all fours. When she extended her arm out in front of her, the light would shine brightly in her eyes, making it difficult to see ahead as it was so dark.

The tunnel curved to her right. She edged around the bend and saw a sliver of natural sunlight shining down. She scampered on her hands and knees.

Nora looked up.

The narrow fracture stretching up to the surface was no bigger than six inches.

She continued on. Her hands were getting sore and scraped from the rough rock, which was also killing her knees.

The underground passageway was now a mere crawlspace, and getting narrower as she struggled through. Soon, she was on her belly, using her flat elbows to pull herself over the ground and pushing off with the toes of her boots.

She kept wondering if she should turn back. But at this point, it seemed impossible because she would have to squirm her way backward. She knew if she did manage to get back, she would be stuck in the same situation, and still wouldn't be able to climb out.

Proceeding ahead was the only alternative.

But what if she got stuck? She had never been prone to claustrophobia, but then, she had never been in this dire of a situation before.

She flashed on a movie she'd watched with Jake one evening, called *The Descent*.

A small group of women had gone spelunking in an unexplored cave system, unaware that there were flesh-eating troglodytes lurking in the subterranean passages. It had been an especially creepy movie, as the cave dwellers were blind as bats but had keen hearing, which they relied on to detect their prey.

She remembered one particular, intense scene, when the women were trying to fit through a tight crawlspace, the threat always looming that they might get stuck or be buried alive in the event of a cave-in.

It was one thing watching that movie, but it was another actually living it.

Because now she was in a similar situation as she crawled further, having to stretch her arms out in front of her, so too narrow her shoulders. She had to use her stomach muscles, like a snake, to inch herself forward.

Genuine panic was beginning to set in. She could feel her heart beating, like a hummingbird trapped in a glass jar, thumping in her chest.

She had to calm down or she would have a panic attack.

Nora closed her eyes. She took controlled breaths. She thought of Jake, and a time they had gone on a short vacation. She'd found this great deal—Acapulco for three days and two nights, including airfare—incredibly cheap.

She should have heeded her mother's old saying, "You get what you pay for."

It had been the vacation in hell.

Acapulco was sweltering, hundred-degree weather. On the very first day, they had gotten trapped in a stalled outdoor elevator with a car full of other tourists. As the lift had malfunctioned, the overhead fan had turned off. They were baking inside and could see people below, enjoying the swimming pool. When they'd pounded on the glass for help, the people in their bathing suits only looked up and waved. Everyone inside the elevator was dripping with sweat by the time the hotel staff came to the rescue.

Instead of the pool, they decided to go to the beach.

Jake had suggested a shortcut down an alley. He quickly changed his mind when he saw lurking figures checking them out. They took the long way around, only to find armed soldiers patrolling the beach, which made them uncomfortable, so they went back to their hotel.

That night, they went out to go to a nightclub. Not really sure where they were going, Jake pointed to some concrete steps leading up to the front of a single-story building. Jake had taken her hand and they'd raced up the steps like a couple of high school teenagers.

A menacing-looking soldier with an automatic rifle was sitting on the stoop.

It was then they realized that the building wasn't a nightclub but an official government office.

They'd backed down the stairs and spent the evening drinking margaritas and doing tequila shots in a small hole-in-the-wall bar.

The next day, they'd gone out on a three-tier excursion boat to enjoy a relaxing bay cruise.

There were about three hundred people on board, scattered about the three decks.

The crew had set up tables with paper plates and plastic cups, as food and drinks were to be served.

An unexpected monsoon hammered the vessel. The winds were so strong, that they scooped everything off the tables and sent them over the side. The torrential rain blew in sidewise across the decks soaking the passengers, which caused everyone to panic and run to the opposite side of the ship. The sudden shift in weight of three hundred people caused the ship to take a drastic list. Nora was certain that they were going to capsize.

To top it off, the only life preserver on the boat was a wooden one, mounted on the bulkhead.

On their last day, Jake and Nora were carrying their luggage down the hall to the elevator just around the corner. The elevator door was open. Nora was about to step in, when Jake pulled her back.

The car wasn't there. She'd almost fallen down the elevator shaft. She gazed at the long cables stretching down and saw the roof of the elevator car, fourteen floors below.

It was one vacation they would never forget, but at least they'd survived and walked away with stories to tell.

Nora wondered if she would be sharing her experiences of Desolation National Park.

She certainly hoped so.

Her clothes were grimy and damp from crawling through the tunnel. She was chilled to the bone. Her teeth began to chatter but only briefly.

Nora snagged her sleeve on a sharp rock, and as she tried to pull away, she accidentally severed the plastic tubing around the copper core wire, damaging the electroluminesence and casting her into utter darkness.

She reached over to activate the other sleeve then stopped when she saw a pinprick of light farther ahead.

It had to be the mouth of a cave. She was certain of it.

The passage became bigger, enabling Nora to get on her hands and knees, and continue with a renewed sense of hope. She wanted to call out to Jake, tell him that she had found a way out, but decided to wait until she could give him the proper instructions to her whereabouts.

Nora edged out of the tunnel onto a three-foot wide ledge. She was about ten feet under the ceiling of an enormous glacier cavern. Limestone stalactites hung overhead and looked like wax drippings.

The walls were covered with patches of lime-green lichen that glowed, illuminating the cavern like a giant subdued nightlight.

She heard the fluttering of tiny wings and looked up. She was right under a large colony of sleeping bats. They were flush up against one another. Maybe that was how they stayed warm, sharing body heat. A few of the creatures were repositioning themselves during slumber.

She looked down in front of her and saw that the ledge was covered in guano. She got on her knees and quietly wiped her hands off on her pants.

Nora leaned over and looked down into the wet grotto. It was a fifty-foot drop down to the cavern floor, which spanned more than half the area of a football field. An abundant number of stalagmites had formed throughout the centuries. A large pond of crystal clear water was in a large, turquoise-bottom granite bowl the size of a public swimming pool.

Thirty snake-like creatures wriggled on the surface. Judging from the distance, they had to be at least four feet long.

She glanced about the terrain below and realized that the entire cavern floor was teeming with centipedes—like the one that had killed Gail—only larger.

Much larger.

Her heart raced again, like it did when she almost had the panic attack back in the tunnel. She closed her eyes and took a couple deep breaths. It was difficult not to be scared out of her mind, but she knew if she was going to get out of this place alive, she had to keep her cool.

She opened her eyes and looked back down.

At first, it looked like a humongous orgy with over a hundred centipedes crawling over one another. As she studied the layout of the cavern floor, she soon discovered that there was a purpose to it all.

She watched a five-foot long centipede crawl into a depression. It undulated its body, and after a moment, it scrambled out of the recess. Nora saw that it had left a wet deposit of spunk.

Another centipede crawled into the same hole and coiled its body to rest inside.

She counted more than twenty centipedes spiraled in tight coils in similar cavities.

They were breeding.

In another section of the hatchery, a score of centipedes were giving birth to clusters of white eggs that looked like giant cocktail onions the size of tennis balls.

A centipede charged into one of the nests and grabbed an egg with its front pinchers. The mother centipede attacked the intruder and they fought, biting one another and grappling with their strong legs. They twisted and rolled about in the small pit in a fierce scuffle.

Soon, the interloper became still.

As sick as it was to watch the confrontation, Nora still felt good that the mother centipede had won the fight.

That was until the mother centipede began eating her own eggs.

Nora turned away and looked over at another area where larger centipedes were feeding on smaller ones—cannibals feeding on their own kind.

Nora heard something moving about below, something massive.

She looked down and saw a grotesque head appear out of a side passage, followed by an enormous segmented body. It easily dwarfed the other centipedes. Nora kept watching as it made its appearance. Just when she thought it had completely exited the passage, its body continued.

Finally, the rear section swished out.

Nora stared aghast.

The thing had to be twenty feet long.

The gigantean centipede climbed over the sprawl of writhing bodies on its powerful legs. It passed by a wall where another behemoth centipede was completing the last stage of moulting, and was squirming out of its empty exoskeleton. Its cuticle was soft and pale, making it appear vulnerable.

Nora figured in a short time the new skin would harden into a protective shell.

She continued to watch the twenty-foot-long centipede cross the cavern floor. It passed three craters in the rock where three other thick-body centipedes were curled up in a spiral ball, forming a circle that had to be ten feet in diameter. A few eggs had shifted to the outer perimeter and were visible. The white spheres were the size of melons.

Shrill shrieks echoed in the cavernous underground chamber. Nora looked up and saw that the ceiling was a turbulent frenzy. The bats were going in all directions as though their sonar had malfunctioned and they were flying blind. Many of the bats smashed headfirst into the cavern walls like misdirected kamikaze pilots.

The sound was so piercing that Nora had to cover her ears.

Something caught in her hair near the top of her scalp.

She reached up to brush away the bat. It wrapped around a few strands and tugged violently like it wanted to rip out her hair.

Nora looked up. It wasn't a bat.

It was a centipede, hanging from the ceiling.

She scooted back to get away. Another centipede clawed at her, tearing a hole in her jacket. She gazed up at the ceiling. It was crawling with centipedes. They were clinging to the rock by their hind legs, snatching bats out of the air as they flew by.

Nora drew her jacket hood up over her head and curled up in a ball, unable to escape the mad frenzy.

CHAPTER THIRTY

Ally slipped into her Dri-Fit shirt that hugged her upper torso like a second skin.

She grabbed her spandex running pants, sat on the edge of the bed, and slipped her stocking feet into the legs, pulling the tight-fitting pants up around her waistline.

She went into her closet and pulled down a shoebox off the shelf. She opened the lid and took out a brand new pair of running shoes. She had been wearing them around the house to break them in and decided it was time to put them to the test on an actual run.

After she had threaded the laces and put on the shoes, she jumped up and down to see if they had spring in them. They were a little stiff, but she figured after a couple good runs, the shoes would soften up.

Her room was a monument of her athletic accomplishments. A bookshelf took up one wall in her room and was completely filled with trophies and various awards she had received participating in track and field. Most of which she had taken first place; there were very few second and third places.

Posters of her favorite sports figures and idols hung on the other three walls.

Florence Griffith Joyner ran proudly wearing number 569 after a victorious race, her arms in the air as she smiled, the caption: "I believe in the impossible because no one else does."

Allyson Felix stood in a red track uniform with her name Felix banded across her chest; her arms spread wide holding the stars and stripes behind her.

Natasha Hastings powered down the track in a 400-meter race.

There were some nostalgic graphics of past Olympic venues throughout the past years.

Next year, she would be a senior. She hoped her excellent achievements in track and field might earn her a college scholarship and unburden her mother from having to get a loan from the bank to pay for the outrageous fees that colleges were expecting students to pay for tuitions.

Ally left her bedroom and skipped down the stairs into the living room. Dillon and Rochelle were on the couch. Winston was curled up by the coffee table, taking a nap.

Dillon looked up from his comic book.

"Where're you going?" he asked.

"Out for a run. Where's Ryan?"

"In the barn."

"Working on his car?"

"I think so."

"I shouldn't be long. If you need anything, you know where Ryan is. I'll be less than an hour. Okey dokey?"

"Okey dokey."

Ally went over to Winston and tapped his left thigh gently with the toe of her running shoe.

The bull terrier opened one sleepy eye, and gazed up.

"Winston, you're in charge."

The bull terrier immediately scrambled to his feet. Whenever anyone told Winston he was in charge, he immediately assumed it was a direct command.

Winston marched over and sat down on the throw rug at Dillon's feet.

"Good boy." Ally looked at Dillon. "I'll be back in a flash."

Dillon smiled and went back to his DC Kids comic.

Ally made sure she had her mobile phone and house key tucked in the pockets of her skinny pants. She went out the backdoor from the kitchen and walked across the mudroom. She swung open the outside door and ran down the steps onto a patch of grass.

Before her run, she limbered up with some stretches. She sat on the ground and extended her right leg first. She leaned forward as far as she could stretch and touched the toe of her shoe. After ten repetitions, she did the same with the left leg.

She stood up, put her hands on her hips, and leaned side to side at the waist.

Once she felt she had warmed up her muscles sufficiently, she took off down the gravel driveway at a slow pace and turned onto the asphalt road.

Normally, she would wear a pedometer clipped to her waistband, but today, she decided not to. She had run up and down the same country roads and trails so many times she had mentally gauged their distances.

Ally knew where to run in order to attain the degree of workout she desired, and today, it would be a moderate jog, as she was breaking in a new pair of running shoes.

She started off at an even pace, slow enough so as not to tire too soon, but at a steady enough clip to ensure a decent workout. She wished she'd worn thicker socks as she could feel the back of her shoes rubbing on her heels, which if she weren't careful, would create blisters.

Blisters to a runner were like broken fingers to a pianist.

Ahead was a good long stretch of roadway that ran through the woods with enough incline to guarantee a good burn in her thighs and calves. The return trip was even better as it was downhill and enabled her to exercise different muscles in her forelegs and shins.

She kept a steady pace for the first leg of the run. Reaching a barbwire post on the side of the road, she broke into a fast sprint, running like she was competing in a track tournament. She poured it on, pumping her arms. Her legs were on fire.

Once she reached the stop sign at the junction of the road, Ally slowed up and came to a staggering halt. She'd measured the distance between the post and the sign once when she'd worn her pedometer.

She had just completed a 100-meter dash.

It was a shame she hadn't brought along her stopwatch as she thought the run might have been one of her personal best, even with new shoes.

Ally looked down, noticing that the shoelace on her right shoe had come undone. She certainly didn't want to step on it and trip on the hard asphalt.

She'd taken a bad fall once running high hurdles and had skinned herself up pretty bad on the all-weather running track. The hard rubber and asphalt composite was like skidding on coarse sandpaper.

Just like a boxer that was always cautious to his surroundings in the ring, Ally was always careful when running down hills or on wet surfaces. Tripping on her own shoelaces and taking a spill was just plain inexcusable.

Ally stepped off the asphalt onto the dirt shoulder so as not to get run over by any cars coming down the road even though she hadn't seen one vehicle since she had left the farmhouse.

She went down on her left knee with her right foot out in front of her. She was about to form two loops when she heard a rustling.

Nora glanced over at the field of tall grass by the side of the road. It was difficult to tell if there was an animal lurking unseen as the vegetation was rippling under a gentle breeze.

She finished tying her shoe and stood.

A white mail truck stopped on a parallel road on the other side of the field.

Jackson Tucker climbed out and waved his arms. "Ally, is that you?" he shouted.

"Oh boy," Ally mumbled to herself. "Yes, Mr. Tucker," she hollered back.

"I got your mail if you want to come over and get it."

It was always the same old thing. Every time their postman got the opportunity, he'd find ways to shorten his route; get his customers to accept their mail whenever he bumped into them, whether they were pushing a shopping cart coming out of the market or taking a leisurely stroll walking their pet.

Ally hated cutting through that field. She knew she'd pick up burrs that would stick to her socks and get inside her new shoes. Some of the burrs were so tiny they would even get entangled in the shoelaces and would be a bear to remove.

She thought about politely declining and given Mr. Tucker a lame excuse that she was in a big hurry to get home, but that would have been a lie. As much as she hated to cross the field, she decided she didn't have any other choice.

"I'm coming over," Ally shouted.

She waded into the tall grass, which was just up to her waist. It had once been a cornfield before it was plowed over a couple of years ago. The ground was uneven and clumpy in spots.

Ally wasn't halfway across when her right foot squished down into something wet and mushy. She looked down and saw that she had trod into some animal's excrement—in her brand new shoes. The brown patty oozed up over the toe of her shoe.

She wanted to scream and go yell at Mr. Tucker, but she kept her temper.

Something slithered in the grass to her right.

During the warmer months, diamondback rattlesnakes would come down from the higher elevations to the valley were it was cooler. Ally remembered when her mom had discovered a six-footer coiled under their front porch steps poised to strike at the first person that might come down the stairs. Her mom had gotten her Remington pump and shot it.

Afterward, Ryan had been tasked repairing a few of the steps, as they had been riddled and blasted apart by the buckshot.

She continued on to outdistance whatever it was, and heard something move about in the grass to her left. This sound was becoming increasingly louder which meant that the source of the noise was heading in her direction.

Ally burst into a run.

She prayed she didn't stumble into a gopher hole and sprain an ankle. The grass blades whipped against the silky material of her spandex pants as she ran.

She was almost there when she tripped and fell face-first. The fall had almost knocked the wind out of her. She looked back and saw that she had stumbled over an old log.

The slithering grew louder.

Ally turned her head.

It was scurrying straight for her.

She screamed with fear.

A brown rat ran past and darted into the thick stalks.

Ally scrambled to her feet and ran, determined that nothing was going to prevent her from getting to safety. She cleared the tall grass and climbed up the short embankment to where the mail truck was parked.

"You sure put on a show," Mr. Tucker said. "Thought you were being chased by a swarm of yellow jackets. Even had my Mace ready." He showed her the pepper spray can then stuffed it back in a pouch on his belt.

Ally bent down and put her hands on her knees, trying to catch her breath. She looked down at her new shoes. They were badly soiled and covered with thistles and burrs just like she had feared. She looked up at the mailman.

He could tell she was upset.

"Well, let me get your mail out of my bin." Mr. Tucker went to the driver's side and reached across the seat. He pulled out a bundle of mail and sorted through it.

"Let me see, here's your copy of *Track and Field News*." He handed Ally the magazine. "Looks like Ryan got something from the Department of Motor Vehicles. Probably registration on that fancy car of his."

Ally hated the way he scrutinized everyone's mail. She wondered if he had ever heard of invasion of privacy. Her mom once joked that those coke-bottle glasses he wore were actually X-ray, which enabled him to secretly read everyone's mail, still sealed in the envelopes.

The mailman looked at the next few pieces of correspondence. "Got something from the phone company. Here's one from a Stanford University."

Ally's ears perked up when she heard the mention of the college.

He handed her the mail. "Well, that's about it."

Mr. Tucker climbed into the Jeep mail truck. He started up the engine and gave her a wave. "See you later. Got a lot more mail to deliver."

Ally watched the vehicle drive off, and soon it disappeared around a bend in the road.

She looked over at the field. If she went back across, she could be home in fifteen minutes. If she stayed on this road, it would take her at least forty-five minutes as it went back behind the hills before it looped around to where she lived.

Ally started a slow jog down the road.

CHAPTER THIRTY-ONE

Donny Decker pulled his forty-ton 18-wheeler big rig into the parking area next to the feed store. He had to make a wide turn then straightened out the bobtail truck tractor's fifty-five-foot trailer. He pressed his boot down on the brake pedal and the air-braking system let out a loud hiss.

Checking his mirrors, Donny double-clutch shifted into reverse. He slowly backed up, aligning the back of the trailer with the rollup door on the side of the feed store. Once he was satisfied that he was in position, he shut down the beastly Mack truck's 605 horsepower engine.

He grabbed a clipboard with the appropriate shipping advices. He opened the driver's door, grabbed a handle, and stepped down out of the cab.

Donny had been an independent trucker for almost fifteen years. He'd picked up his trailer for forty grand, the tractor for another eighty thousand dollars, which had put him deep in the red. He'd put in so many hours on the road, just to keep up the payments, that it had cost him his marriage.

Luckily, they hadn't had any kids—the child support would have drained him dry—and his wife hadn't been vindictive soaking him for alimony. She was a good person but needed the company of a man that was willing to give her more of his time than what Donny could provide being on the road three hundred days out of the year.

Like many jobs, Donny had been a victim of his profession. He'd put on a lot of weight due to his sedentary occupation sitting for long hours behind the wheel, and eating greasy food at the truck stops.

Not even the occasional lot lizard could help him burn off calories. He had a potbelly that stretched the front of his shirt and hung out over his beltline. He'd grown a beard, and let his hair grow, sporting a ponytail.

As he spent most nights in the sleeping compartment in the rear of his tractor truck, he was scraggly looking, and was often smelly, as personal hygiene was not a priority. Such was the life of an independent trucker.

He recognized the owner of the feed store, Harmon, as the man came out to greet him.

"Hey, Donny. How's it going?"

"Just fine, Harmon. Got your normal shipment."

"How about that special order?"

Donny leafed through the shipping advice copies that he would be handing over to Harmon.

"Yep, it's right here."

"Good deal. That one's for our sheriff."

"Mighty pricey for dog food."

"It's the only brand her dogs will eat."

"Must be that Kobe beef," Donny said. "Her pets eat better than I do. Any chance you know where I could grab a bite?"

"You might try the Log Jam Diner across the street." Donny looked at the small eatery.

"Any good?" he asked.

"No one's complained yet."

"Okay then." Donny handed Harmon his copies and went around to the back of the trailer. He unlocked the padlock and raised a bar, setting it in a slot. He swung open the left door and pushed it around on its hinges so that it was flat against the side of the trailer where he hooked it so it wouldn't swing out. He did the same with the right door.

"You got yourself a load there," Harmon said, looking inside the trailer.

Two rows of pallets stretched all the way back to the front of the fifty-five footer. A pallet jack was wedged up under a front pallet so that Donny could jockey the pallets inside the trailer.

"Those first two pallets are yours. The rest I'm taking to Oakland to be shipped overseas."

"Let me get my lift." Harmon walked back inside the feed store. His yellow forklift was parked against the wall. The rear panel was open. A connector cable stretched from the battery down to the charger.

Harmon unhooked the cable. He closed the panel. The driver's seat was tilted forward, a feature that assured that whenever anyone stepped from the equipment, the electric motor would be disengaged.

He climbed up, pushed the seat back, and sat on it. He pulled back the lever on the steering column to put the forklift in reverse and pressed on the foot pedal.

Nothing happened.

"What the heck?"

Harmon tried it again, but the lift didn't move.

He jumped down and inspected the charger. It was plugged in, but the light wasn't shining. He fidgeted with the plug in the wall socket and the light came on.

"Damn socket's faulty."

He came out and looked up at Donny, who was standing inside the trailer.

"My lift didn't charge. We're going to have to break down the pallets and offload by hand."

"Well, that's screwed up," Donny said. He climbed down and almost fell.

"Whoa," Harmon said, and grabbed the trucker's arm to steady the man.

"Thanks, Harmon." Donny pulled up on the lip and began pulling out the ramp tucked under the bed of the truck.

"Here, let me help you with that," Harmon offered, and grabbed one side as they stretched the ramp out and dropped the end on the ground.

"You got a box cutter?" Donny asked.

"Sure do. You know, Donny, if you want to go eat, be my guest. It's going to take me awhile to lug those bags into the store."

"I don't know, Harmon. I should keep an eye on my rig."

"You can do that from across the street. Just ask Peggy for a window seat."

"Sure you don't want any help?"

"No, I'm good. Besides, this is my fault, and you shouldn't have to suffer."

"Well, thank you, Harmon. I think I'm going to take you up on that. Hey, you don't have a customer restroom I could use?"

"It's over there," Harmon said and pointed to the blue portable toilet at the rear of the building.

"Thanks."

Donny went down to the porta-potty and stepped inside. He unzipped his fly and peed in the toilet. He wrinkled his nose at the smell, wondering when the last time someone had pumped the tank.

He zipped up and stepped out, not bothering to close the door properly, figuring the latrine could use a good airing out.

***

Harmon was working up a sweat offloading the feedbags.

When he first started, he'd been carrying two fifty-pound bags at a time down the ramp and into the store. But after he was through clearing off the first pallet, and had stacked the wooden transport structure up against the wall, he realized that he couldn't continue at that pace if he didn't want to burn himself out.

He continued on, hefting a single bag over his shoulder, keeping it up for nearly thirty minutes. He had just finished bringing in the last sack when Maxine came into the warehouse from the rear entry that led back into their adjacent home.

"Harmon? Care for some lunch?"

Harmon tossed the sack down on the pile of feedbags.

"What are we having?"

"Your favorite."

"Best let me wash up."

"Don't dally or it'll get cold."

"I won't."

Harmon walked out and looked across the street. He could see Donny through the front window of the diner, sitting at a window seat. He was eating his lunch. The truck driver looked up and saw Harmon, and gave him a wave with a fork in his hand.

Harmon waved back. He pointed to the clipboard that Donny had left in the back of the trailer. He took the pen that was wedged in the clip and showed it to Donny, making a writing motion.

Donny nodded that he understood and went back to his meal.

Harmon signed Donny's shipping advice copies and went inside for his own lunch.

***

Peggy, the waitress, wasn't what you would call a looker, but she sure had a sweet smile.

The second Donny had walked in the diner, she was waiting by the cash register with a menu in her hand.

"Hey, there. Welcome to the Log Jam."

"Well, thank you," Donny replied, liking her already. He hoped the name of the diner wasn't any reference to how he would feel later after a hearty meal. The one thing he hated worse than the screaming shits when he was doing a long haul was suffering from constipation and not being able to take a healthy crap.

"Where would you like to sit?" It was an honest question as there were no other customers in the tiny restaurant.

"I need to keep an eye on my rig across the street, so I'd need a table by the front window."

"No problem. Care for some coffee?"

"Sure, coffee would be good."

"Go pick your table and I'll be right with you." Peggy handed Donny a menu.

Donny walked by a couple tables to the one by the window. He pulled out a chair and sat down. He browsed through the menu.

Peggy came right over with his cup of coffee and a glass of water.

"See anything that strikes your fancy," she asked, holding her notepad and pen. She was dressed casually in a white blouse cut low enough to show just a little cleavage, and a pair of tight-fitting jeans. She was wearing a comfortable-looking pair of black sneakers.

"Is it too late for breakfast?"

"Honey, you can have whatever you want."

Donny looked up from the menu and smiled, wondering if Peggy was coming on to him or if that was just her friendly personality.

"What do you recommend?" he asked, keeping the conversation going, hoping that she would give him a hint of her intentions.

"You look like a fellow with a big appetite. How about the Gold Miner's Special?"

Donny didn't know if he should take offense, but didn't want to say anything that might come off defensive, and hurt his chances of maybe scoring a quickie in the back of his cab.

"What's it come with?"

"You get a short stack of buttermilk pancakes dripping with maple syrup, three country fried eggs, two thick strips of Canadian bacon, four slices of sourdough toast, hash browns smothered in brown gravy, a complimentary glass of freshly squeezed orange juice, and for dessert, a wedge of the pie of your choice with a large dollop of whip cream or vanilla ice cream. How's that sound?"

"You sure know how to whet a man's appetite."

"Well, never heard that one before. But they do say that the best way to a man's heart is through his stomach." Peggy winked and scribbled on her pad. "I'll go place your order."

She walked off and went behind the counter. She hung Donny's ticket on a small turnstile in the pass-through for the cook. He was burly with a beard and was wearing a disposable white paper hat.

Donny glanced out the window and saw Harmon carrying a sack over his shoulder, coming down the ramp. The man looked a little spent.

He was half done drinking his coffee when Peggy placed the large plate of food in front of him. He looked down in amazement. It looked as good as it smelled.

"There you go, honey."

"This sure looks delicious."

"Enjoy." Peggy smiled and sauntered back over to the serving counter.

Donny dug in. The yolks were runny just the way he liked them. He had no qualms letting the syrup blend with the gravy. The bacon was a little salty, but he didn't mind.

He looked up from his plate and glanced across the road. Harmon was standing at the back of the trailer. He was pointing at the clipboard.

Donny raised his fork and waved back that he understood. He watched Harmon sign off on the shipping advices and then he placed the clipboard in the back of the trailer. The feed storeowner walked into the warehouse.

Donny was mopping up the last of the gravy on his plate with a piece of toast when Peggy came to his table to see how he was doing.

"Ready for your pie?" she asked.

"I think I have room," Donny replied, dabbing his mouth with a paper napkin.

"Well, we have quite the selection. They're freshly made everyday by a local bakery. They've even won a few first-prize ribbons at the county fair. The pies are in the display case behind the counter, if you care to come over and pick what you want."

Donny glanced across the road at his big rig, which was the only vehicle in the parking lot. He looked up and down the street and didn't see anyone. It looked safe enough.

A thought struck him. Maybe the cook was gone and this was Peggy's way of getting him to go in the back with her.

"Sure, let's see what you have," Donny said, getting up from the table and following the waitress.

*****

They came down off the hill and flooded onto the parking lot like an incoming tide. Most of the centipedes bunched together and ran along the outside wall of the feed store.

One centipede, a three-footer, split off from the scourge and skittered under the door that had been left ajar in the portable toilet.

A small band scampered into the feed store.

The main surge made a beeline for the ramp leading up to the inside of the trailer.

Their size ranged from eighteen inches to four feet in length. They jostled up the ramp into the trailer, scuttling between the boards under the pallets.

They made a loud commotion scurrying about, squeezing under the shrink-wrap stretched over the pallets, and burrowing into the feedbags.

After a moment, the inside of the trailer became eerily quiet.

They were settled in.

***

Donny had purposely dawdled looking at all the different flavored pies. He was biding his time, hoping that Peggy would give him a signal or come up with an excuse to go in the back—maybe to see more pies—and if he would be interested in accompanying her.

But that never happened. Instead, Peggy grew impatient and finally said, "I know, they all look good, but they're not going to pick themselves."

He'd been studying the pies and glancing over his shoulder making sure his rig was okay. From behind the counter, he could only see the tractor truck and about thirty feet of the trailer. He hoped no one was messing with his load.

"I guess I'll have the rhubarb."

"Let me put that on a plate, and I'll bring it right over."

Donny went back to his table. He looked across the street and saw no one near the ramp.

Peggy brought him his pie, a la mode.

He finished the dessert in five bites. He pulled out his wallet and laid a ten-dollar tip on the table. He got up and walked over to the cash register where Peggy was standing.

"Thanks, that hit the spot." Donny handed her a twenty.

"Glad you liked it." Peggy rang him up. The drawer popped out under the register. She reached in to get his change.

"Keep it. Be seeing you," Donny said, expecting her to say likewise, but she just shut the drawer and watched him walk out of the diner. Maybe he'd been too obvious trying to scope her out. Oh well.

He crossed the street.

Donny grabbed the end of the ramp with both hands, lifted with his legs, and walked it up into the slot. He unhooked the left rear door from the side of the trailer and swung it around to the rear. He brought the right rear door around but paused to reach in and grab the clipboard.

He thought he heard something moving around back inside the trailer. He leaned in to listen.

He hoped he hadn't picked up any rats. Last year, he'd picked up a load from a grain store and the bags had been infested with rodents. When Donny had arrived with the shipment, the consignee had refused receipt once the receiving clerk saw the first rat race out of Donny's trailer. It had been a logistic nightmare. The sender claimed that the shipment had been fine when it left their facility and that there must have been rats already in Donny's truck.

His insurance helped out a little, but then they dropped him.

Donny listened for a few moments and was relieved when he didn't hear any noises.

He shut the rear door and threw on the padlock.

He went around to the truck tractor, climbed up, unlocked the driver's door, and climbed up into the driver's seat.

Donny started up the big rig. He pulled around and turned onto the main road.

He blasted his air horn as he drove by the Log Jam Diner.

CHAPTER THIRTY-TWO

Harmon dreaded taking inventory every month, but it had to be done if they were going to keep their records straight for their business and be prepared for each annual income tax audit. He'd gotten wiser through the years and developed shortcuts that would speed the process along the next time he had to do an inventory. Generally, the entire audit would take him three to four hours.

He had labeled the pallets of feedbags that were still shrink-wrapped and hadn't been broken down with the total number of bags that had been on the shipping advice upon receipt. This way, he didn't have to individually count each bag. Math had never been his strong suit. Often, he would have to add up the number of bags on a pallet twice, sometimes even three times, each time getting a different count.

Usually, if he'd been at it for too long, his mind wouldn't work right, and he'd get surly.

Maxine usually didn't assist with the inventory as it gave her a headache. She was always prone to migraines. The ailment had always run in her family. Her mother and grandmother had both suffered from the affliction. She'd tried various treatments and a sundry of pharmaceutical drugs, but nothing really seemed to give her relief. Sometimes the stabbing pain in the back of her head would last for days and she would be laid up in bed.

Today was no exception.

She'd already taken three aspirins, but so far, the medication was slow to kick in.

Harmon stabbed the keys on his handheld calculator with his fat fingers. "Add you dumb thing, not multiplication." He cocked his arm back like he was going to throw the plastic device, and then thought better of it.

"You bust that and you're driving to the Walmart, not me," Maxine said.

"Oh, I get so frustrated at times," Harmon confessed.

"Maybe we should hire someone."

"You know we can't do that. What are we going to pay them with, chicken feed?"

"Well, I wouldn't make a joke about it."

"I was being serious." Harmon belched and rubbed his belly.

"I beg your pardon."

"Sorry, must be your venison stew."

"No one told you to have seconds."

"You know I can't resist good cooking."

"Quit trying to charm me up." Maxine grabbed the back of her skull and clamped her eyes shut.

"Your head again?"

"It's like it's about to come off."

"You know what might help."

"Is that all you think about?" Maxine said, opening her eyes.

"It's worked before."

"What about the inventory?"

"It can wait. I'll drop the rollup doors and put out the 'temporary closed for two hours' sign."

"You mean two minutes."

"You game or not?"

"I'm going to go lie down."

"I take it that's a yes?"

"You can take it however you want," Maxine said and walked through the rear door into the back.

The entry led into a room they used for hanging their aprons, coats, and hats, and there was a place under a tool bench for work boots and shoes.

Maxine slipped off her boots and walked in her stocking feet into the next room, which was their living room. It was small and cozy. They each had their own recliner chairs with end tables for snacks and drinks while they watched their shows on the television across the room. A divan with cushions and a coffee table were on one wall for whenever they had company.

Maxine went into the kitchen.

She opened the tap on the faucet and filled a glass with water. She shook two more aspirins out of the plastic bottle on the counter, and washed them down, ignoring the recommended dosage, as her head was killing her. It was worth casting caution to the wind to be rid of the pain.

She wasn't too worried about the aspirins eating up the lining of her stomach and giving her an ulcer. Unlike, Harmon, she had a cast-iron stomach and loved her hot sauce which was probably why Harmon was ailing, as she had emptied a bottle of the stuff in her venison stew.

She went out of the kitchen and down a hall to their bedroom. She pulled down her dungarees and hung them flat on the back of a chair. She took off her work shirt and draped it over the pants.

Wearing only her bra, a pair of feminine briefs, and her socks, she turned back the covers and climbed into bed. She pushed the blanket back, only using the thin sheet. She sometimes found that pressure on her body made her head hurt even more. It was probably just her way of thinking and there was no medical reason for it.

She'd left the overhead light off. Keeping the room quiet and dark usually helped.

Maxine turned on her side and closed her eyes.

She may have drifted off, she wasn't sure, when she heard something move about in the room. Harmon knew not to make any noise. He was good about that. He knew she was in pain and didn't want to be the cause of making it worse.

But, on the other hand, her husband never missed an opportunity for sex. Even though the act itself was jarring, afterward Maxine had to admit she felt somewhat better and the headache had subsided. Maybe releasing a little stress was the answer.

She felt the sheet rustle by her stocking feet.

A sharp jab in her calf made her flinch.

"Harmon, you best cut those toenails."

Her entire leg was suddenly seized by needle pricks. The stabbings compressed around her knee like a vise.

Maxine turned over and sat up. She threw back the sheet.

It was dark, but she could still see the thing wrapped around her leg.

The pain was intense at first, robbing her mind of her migraine, but then the acute discomfort subsided as if she had just been given a shot of novocaine.

She might have screamed, called out to Harmon to come to her rescue, summoning her knight in shining armor but that was going to be impossible.

Because now she was trying to pull another creature off her face that had been hiding under her pillow. It was wrapping its body around her head. Tiny claws dug viciously into her face and scalp.

The thing was suffocating her.

***

Instead of gradually pulling on the chain that would lower the rollup door, Harmon gave it a quick tug, which caused the chain to jump off the pulley. "Damn it, that's what I get." He'd been in a rush and forgot how temperamental the apparatus was.

Harmon walked over and grabbed the eight-foot ladder. He brought it over and propped it up under the opening so that he could climb up and loop the chain back on the pulley.

He got halfway up the ladder when his stomach did a flip-flop. That's what he called it whenever he had a stomachache, which lately he'd been having more often. He hadn't seen the doctor, as he was afraid what the physician might tell him.

He came down off the ladder. It felt like his insides had joined the circus and were doing a series of somersaults. He was breaking out in a cold sweat. A sharp pain knifed his side.

Harmon knew he only had a few seconds before his bowels unleashed. He could chance running across the feed store and ducking into the house, but he knew he'd never make it in time. He looked outside at the side parking area. Just to the rear of the building was the portable toilet, the small latrine constructed of blue heavy-duty plastic with a gray roof.

He had posted a sign on the door when they had first had it put back there: For Customers Only, which he always thought was a hoot.

The last person to use it had left the damn door open, something that always infuriated him.

Harmon's stomach started gurgling.

He scrambled down the side of the building, unbuckling his pants, trying not to drop his drawers too soon should he stumble and fall, and make a fool of himself. He prayed a customer wouldn't pull into the parking area and see him racing comically to the outdoor latrine.

Harmon stepped into the porta-potty and spun around, letting his trousers fall down over his boots. He reached out and slammed the door closed.

He sat on the seat covering the chemical toilet tank in the nick of time.

Maxine's fine venison stew exploded down into the crapper pit.

"Oh, never again," he moaned, doing a rocking motion. His face was beaded with sweat. Without warning, his bowels opened up again, making a loud splash below.

It was dark inside the portable toilet, as he had mistakenly posted a part of the sign on the other side of the door over a portion of the thinner plastic that was supposed to allow some degree of outdoor light to shine inside. He reached around for the toilet paper roll, but when he found it, there was only the paperboard core on the dispenser.

"Oh isn't that just dandy," he grumbled.

Something sloshed around in the crapper pit.

"What the hell?"

Harmon spread his thighs apart to peek down. It was too dark to really see anything. The smell was enough to knock him out.

He heard a clicking coming up the inside wall of the plastic tank, like someone drumming their fingernails nervously on a hard surface.

Something bit him on the backside.

"Jesus Almighty!" Harmon screamed.

Then it squeezed up between his butt cheeks.

His mind flashed to the time his doctor had referred him to a proctologist to have his prostrate examined. The physician had been wearing a lubricated latex glove and had only inserted one finger—not rammed him with a spiked glove.

He tried to stand but fell back on the toilet seat.

He could feel it burrowing up inside him though it was the strangest thing.

There was no pain.

His legs had gone completely numb. It was like the time he had his wisdom teeth removed, and the dentist had shot his mouth up with a local anesthesia and he couldn't feel a thing. He felt almost euphoric as he slipped into unconsciousness.

CHAPTER THIRTY-THREE

Twice, Jake had nearly fallen off the narrow ledge that angled down on the side of the cliff. He tried not to look down at the rocks below, and concentrated on the granite path in front of him, which was only wide enough to place one foot directly in front of the other.

It was like walking a tightrope.

His shoulder throbbed, making matters worse. Before descending down the rock wall, he had applied a fresh dressing to the wound and wrapped duct tape over the bandage to keep it in place so that the adhesive strip sealed the oozing hole and staunched the bleeding.

He stumbled down the last few feet of the stone path onto flat ground. He was wringing wet with sweat. The fear of falling and the exertion was part of it, but he feared that he was coming down with a fever from his wound. He had no idea how much blood he'd lost.

Whenever he'd had blood work done, he was always amazed at how much blood the lab technician would draw, filling up four or five tubes at a time. To him, it always looked like a lot of blood, though the technician would assure him that it wasn't that much, and that he needn't worry.

He tried to think how much blood was in a human body. Of course, that would depend on the size of the person. Was it a gallon? He hoped so. Then he might have some to spare. But by the way he was feeling, that gallon jug had sprung a slow leak, robbing him of his strength, and the more he pushed himself, the weaker he became.

The hatchet felt heavy in his hand, so he tucked the handle down in the side of his pants so that the wood grip was flush with his hip and outer thigh. He'd have to be careful swinging his arm so as not to cut his hand on the sharp blade.

His arm with the injured shoulder hung in a sling that he had formed out of a shirt and was elevated to minimize blood loss.

Jake stumbled over to one of the small lakes and knelt on the hard rock. He scooped his hand in the water and splashed his face. He cupped more water into his palm and drank.

He got back up and saw the path leading into the trees, which would eventually lead to a junction in the trail. He'd follow the fork that ran along the basin and search for an entrance into the side of the mountain.

He prayed that Nora was holding it together, knowing that she had to be scared out of her mind. Being trapped down there, surrounded by nothing but rock.

He trudged over the uneven rocks until he reached the flat path. It was easier, striding over the hard-packed dirt. He picked up his pace and lumbered under the canopy of pine trees. The overhead branches shaded him from the sun.

Up ahead, Jake could see where the trail split into two paths. He hurried the best he could, conscious that if he overexerted himself, he might reopen his wound, and then he wouldn't be any good to Nora or himself.

Jake was stepping around the trunk of a large tree when he stopped dead in his tracks.

Craig sat on a rock next to the trail marker. He looked deathly ill. His face was ashen. The bandage wrapped around his mutilated hand was soaked with blood.

The Colt revolver was in his other hand, pointed down at the ground.

He glared at Jake. "Thought I'd killed you, Carver."

"Not a chance."

Craig raised the heavy handgun and put it on his knee.

"You know what I did with that meddling wife of yours?"

"I know, you bastard." Keeping partially concealed behind the tree, Jake slowly pulled the hatchet from his waistband. He hung the blade on a knob protruding from the trunk.

"Step away from the tree."

"Why, so you can shoot me?"

"That's the plan."

"How could you be so heartless? Treating Gail the way you did."

Craig laughed. "I was going to leave her anyway. You see, Jakey boy, I've been tucking money away from the business for some time. I even bought a nice little chalet in Tahoe, right on the lake. Of course, Gail knew nothing about it. Stupid woman. That thing, whatever it was, did me a favor."

Jake reached up and grabbed the hatchet by the handle.

"Now, I'm not going to tell you again. Step away from the tree." Craig slowly raised the gun barrel.

Jake sidestepped away from the tree and flung the hatchet straight at Craig.

Craig stared at the spinning object flying at his face.

The blade cleaved into his forehead, the impact toppling him backwards off the rock.

Jake walked over and looked down at Craig. His eyes were still open but he was clearly dead.

Kneeling down, Jake searched Craig's pockets. He found the keys to the Bronco and Gail's cell phone.

"Finally, some good luck," Jake said to himself. He pressed a button and the screen lit up. "All right." But as he held the phone up to try and get a signal, a message came on the screen: No Service.

"Damn."

Perhaps if he got to higher ground, he might get a signal and be able to summon help.

But that would have to wait.

He had to find Nora.

He hoped she hadn't crossed paths with any spiders, as they always gave her the willies. And what was that thing that had killed Gail? He had no idea that centipedes could get that big. What was it, three, four feet long? Had to have been a genetic defect of some sort. Nora certainly didn't need to contend with any of those.

She was probably buggy enough trying to find a way out.

***

Nora hadn't moved a muscle in over an hour. She was finding it difficult to breathe, as her jacket hood was pulled tight around her head, but then every time she tried to let in a little dank air, the cloying stench of ammonia would waft up her nostrils, and she would gag.

To make matters worse, she'd been splattered with blood and guano, and was buried under a heap of dead bats. Once in a while, she would hear a pitiful squeak or feel a tiny body shudder.

A few times, centipedes crawled over her like she was just another obstacle in their path, like a rock or a piece of wood, and kept on going. Nora figured being smothered with blood, bat feces, and decomposing bodies, that the centipedes were unable to detect her scent.

Her eyes, along with her nose and throat, were burning from the pungent smell.

She knew she couldn't remain in this position much longer or the fumes would overcome her and she would die.

Very slowly, Nora stretched out her legs. She rolled on her stomach and gradually pushed herself up onto her knees. Dead bats slid off her back and fell onto the ledge, which was covered with clumps of white guano.

She pulled her hood off her head and looked around. Her eyes were tearing, and she was trying desperately not to cough. She glanced up at the ceiling and only saw bare rock as the bats and centipedes were gone.

Nora glanced down at the floor of the cavern. She didn't see any movement.

Remembering how active the centipedes had been earlier, she wondered if she was witnessing their downtime, when they went into a dormant state, perhaps to sleep.

This was her window of opportunity—and might be her only one—and she had to seize it.

Now!

Nora stood, keeping her back against the wall and slowly sidestepped down the ledge. She had to be careful, as the guano-caked rock was slippery, and if she should lose her footing, she'd fall for sure into the midst of the massive colony, awaking the monstrous throng of centipedes.

A single bat swooped silently over the sleeping horde and darted into a passage.

It made perfect sense that the bat would want to distance itself from these predators.

Nora wondered if that was a way out. It had to be.

Reaching that passage meant crossing the cavern floor and walking directly past the gigantic centipede that had recently sloughed off its skin.

She stepped lightly across the rock. Her right boot trod in a small stand of water. She took another step and tried not to make a splash. Gingerly, she waded out of the puddle.

Her left boot came down and made a squishy sound.

Nora froze.

A few of the centipedes stirred.

She took another step and slowly put her foot down. The water-soaked sole made a soft squelch.

The next step was less audible.

She could see the entrance to the tunnel that the bat had flown into.

It was just another fifteen feet. She couldn't believe her luck.

She was almost there…

The Maximus woke up and slowly turned in Nora's direction.

***

Jake stayed close to the base of the ridge, canvassing the granite mountainside for any opening. He had found horizontal fissures, but they had been too narrow for him to squeeze through. One small cave showed promise, but after he crawled inside, he found that it only tunneled in for ten feet then came to a dead end.

He was almost to the summit and was becoming discouraged when he spotted something flying out from behind a large briar bush. It came right at him and flew over his head.

At first, Jake thought it was a small bird, but as he turned to watch it fly away, he realized that it was a bat. Didn't bats only come at night?

He stepped over the loose rock and peered behind the thicket. He could see the shadowy indentation of a cave.

Jake used his hatchet—he'd had to step on Craig's face to pull the ax out of the dead man's skull—and chopped away at the thorny branches, clearing a path to the cave's entrance.

He looked inside and saw a tunnel stretching back into the darkness.

Finally, he'd found a way in.

***

Nora had mere seconds as the gigantic centipede twisted its head to face in her direction. She got down on her belly and rolled into the colossal centipede's heap of molted skin. It was like crawling inside a giant pig rind. The smell was enough to make her pass out. She pinched her nose with her thumb and forefinger, and took shallow breaths through her mouth.

The gigantesque arthropod swept its head over the discarded husk.

Nora cringed as she stared up at the twin pinchers arched inward over the venomous fangs.

The creature's head hovered over her, and just when she thought she could no longer stifle her scream, it turned and rested its head back down on the ground.

Nora gave it another few minutes before she slipped out of the gigantic husk, shrouding herself with a large portion of skin to disguise her scent so that she would blend in.

She entered the passage and crept quietly down the tunnel. She kept looking over her shoulder, praying that they didn't come after her.

Nora was coming around a bend in the tunnel. A dark figure was blocking her way.

"Thank God, you're okay," Jake said.

"Keep your voice down," Nora warned.

"What in the world are you wearing?"

"Never mind that," Nora said, shrugging out of the giant centipede's molted skin. "We have to get out of here. And I mean fast."

"I'm with you."

They hurried down the tunnel, and once when they were outside, they scrambled across the rocks to the dirt path.

By the time they reached the fork in the trail, Jake was having a difficult time keeping up the pace, as his shoulder was acting up.

"I have to stop for a minute," he said.

"You know that thing that killed Gail?"

"Yeah."

"This mountain is full of them. We need to find a way to get help."

"Well, I have this," Jake said, and dug Gail's phone out of his pocket.

"You kook, why didn't you say so?" She grabbed the phone out of Jake's hand and immediately began tapping in the numbers 911.

"You're wasting your time, you won't get a signal."

Nora looked at the screen. "You're right. We have to get to higher ground."

"I do have the keys to the Bronco."

"Better still. We can drive out of here."

"There's no way I can it make down off this mountain," Jake confessed.

"Then it's back to Plan A."

They were just setting out when Nora spotted Craig on the ground by the trail marker. She saw the blood caked on his forehead.

"Is he dead?"

"It was either him or me."

"Guess we won't be shedding any tears for him anytime soon," Nora said as they started up the trail.

CHAPTER THIRTY-FOUR

Donny checked the gauges on the instrument panel. The temperature gauge had crept up a notch toward the red H. The highway up ahead was barricaded by two police cruisers to prevent traffic from entering the lanes littered with broken glass, mangled pieces of metal, and burning flares. A brown van with a crumpled side panel and a white compact sedan with a bashed in front end were blocking the roadway.

He'd been idling for over thirty minutes, watching the emergency crews clear the wreckage. Donny had witnessed the crash from his cab. The van hadn't signaled making a lane change and had swerved in front of the smaller automobile, cutting the other car off.

Donny figured the driver of the van had neglected to check his side mirror.

The driver of the white car couldn't stop in time and rammed into the van's rear bumper, which caused the van to spin sidewise. The white car slammed into the side of the van and both vehicles had come to a screeching halt in the middle of the highway.

If he had a dollar for every reckless driver he'd ever seen in his fifteen years of driving a truck, he'd be a bona fide millionaire.

A patrol car with a heavy-duty brush guard was pushing the van over to the side of the road to clear a lane. A man in an orange jumpsuit was winching the other car up onto a flatbed tow truck.

Donny was relieved when a patrol officer walked over and stood on the white divider line between two open lanes and began flagging the traffic forward.

He checked the clock on the dashboard. He was running a little behind but figured he could make up the lost time, as the road ahead was going to be less congested due to the crash.

He released the air brake, and put the big rig into gear. The semi truck shuddered forward, gradually picking up speed.

The traffic had been sparse, as he had anticipated. He was cruising at 55 miles per hour in the granny lane, the posted speed limit for trucks with trailers. He was reaching in his pocket for a cigarette when he spotted the big digital sign on the side of the road.

Weigh station is open. All trucks must pull in.

"Oh, come on!" Donny downshifted and slowed down. He steered off the main highway and entered the long stretch of pavement leading up to the side of the weigh station building.

A truck hauling even stacks of cut lumber pulled away from the scales.

An inspector was standing by waiting.

Donny drove up and stopped his truck. He leaned his head out the window.

"Freight manifest and logbook," the inspector said in a monotone voice.

Donny handed down the requested paperwork.

The inspector studied the freight manifest as though he were making sure every "i" was dotted and every "t" was crossed properly.

He flipped through the logbook then looked up at Donny. "Better keep a better record of your hours of service. We can't afford you falling asleep on the road."

"Once I'm in Oakland, I'm getting some well-deserved rest."

"See that you do. Let's take a look in the back."

Donny shut down the engine and climbed down from the cab.

He walked behind the inspector as they went to the rear of the trailer. Donny unlocked the padlock and opened the doors.

The inspector shined his flashlight inside.

A few dog food nuggets had spilled out onto the floor from one of the pallets.

"You're not carrying vermin, are you?" the inspector asked.

"No, hell no." He figured Harmon must have moved the pallet jack and accidentally torn one of the bags. "I must have clipped one of the bags with my mover."

"All right. You're good to go." The inspector handed Donny the freight manifest and his logbook.

Donny went around and climbed back up into his cab. He started the engine and pulled away from the weigh station.

In another forty miles, he'd be in Oakland. After he dropped off this load, he had big plans: a hot shower at the nearest Holiday Inn, order up a thick porterhouse steak, wash it down with a case of beer, and catch up on some much-needed sleep.

***

As Jackson Tucker was Prospect's postmaster and only mail carrier, the residents in the small community were forced to put up with his idiosyncrasies. People were always complaining about the limited hours of the post office, which was generally closed in the afternoons while Tucker was out on his route. Some had even volunteered to help out, but Tucker had balked that no one but a government employee was allowed to handle the mail.

He was down to one last bin and decided it was time for a break. He turned off the main thoroughfare near the Rafferty's farmhouse and drove the mail truck up a dirt side road. The Jeep had no problem scaling the incline to the top of the hillock.

Of all the places he would stop taking time off from his work, this was his favorite spot because of the view it afforded him of the mountain range and the forest in Desolation National Park.

Tucker parked the mail truck next to a large mushroom-shaped oak tree. He shut off the engine and walked to the rear of the Jeep. Grabbing the handle, he raised the metal rollup door and sat on the edge of the cargo space.

He opened his lunch box and took out his thermos. He removed the cover that served as a cup and unscrewed the cap. He poured himself some coffee into the cup.

Tucker took a drink and placed the cup on the cargo bed.

He reached inside and grabbed a customer's copy of *Playboy* from the bin. He flipped through the pages, pausing at the juicier photographs. He opened the centerfold page and gawked at the voluptuous naked model with the staple in her belly button.

Finally, he closed the magazine. He made sure that he hadn't creased the corners and the cover was still pristine like it had just come off the press.

He reached behind the bin and got his mini portable plastic bag sealer machine.

Tucker placed the magazine back in its original mailer with the customer's name and address and ran the edge of the machine over the seal, which sucked out the air and sealed the bag.

Good as new.

Why should he subscribe for magazines, when he could read his customers' for free? Surely, there was no harm in that. He never considered himself a scoundrel, but whenever he had to deliver discount coupon fliers, especially the ones that stated that they would only honor the first few shoppers, he often tossed them into the dumpster behind his building, increasing his chances so that he could capitalize on the reduced sales prices.

He was about to jump down from the back of the Jeep when he noticed another magazine he had removed from its original sleeve and needed to reseal.

Tucker laid the plastic sleeve on the cargo floor, and lifted the magazine out of the bin.

A breeze blew the plastic covering out of the back of the Jeep.

"Oh, darn," Tucker said and jumped down. The mailman ran frantically to catch the clear magazine cover.

The wind swept the plastic sleeve behind the thick trunk of the oak tree.

Tucker tripped over a gopher hole and went sprawling onto the ground. His glasses flew off his face.

He reached all around, searching for his glasses. He was blind as a bat without them. He tried not to panic. What would he do if he couldn't find them? He would be stranded. No one would think to look for him here.

But what if he got back in the Jeep and started beeping the horn? Surely, someone would hear him.

He continued to scramble about the ground, feeling around, but he wasn't having any luck finding his spectacles.

Without his glasses, all he could see were blurry, shadowy shapes.

In front of him was a very dark mass. He crawled towards it.

His fingers dug into loose dirt. He reached down, in what appeared to be a very large hole in the ground, far too big to be a gopher hole.

Something grabbed his hand and pulled him underground.

***

Deputy Arness Monroe drove by the sheriff's farmhouse. He was heading back to the office. He happened to look up at the knoll, where a lot of the teenagers liked to go and make out, and spotted Jackson Tucker's mail truck parked by the oak tree.

The deputy had been expecting a new charger for his iPhone, and thought he should drive up and ask Jackson if there was a package for him back at the post office.

He steered the cruiser up the steep road and parked next to the Jeep.

Deputy Monroe got out of his car and left the driver's door open. He walked over to the mail truck. He looked up front and came around to the back.

"Jackson! Where'd you go?" he called out.

No answer.

He thought it was odd that Jackson would just walk off and leave his mail truck open and unattended. The mailman was always a stickler when it came to the rules and regulations governing his duties.

Maybe the truck broke down, and Jackson was down on the main road trying to get a lift back into town so that he could get Dale at the Arco to give him a tow.

Deputy Monroe took his cell phone out of his pocket and called the filling station.

Dale picked up after the third ring. "Dale's Arco, what can I do for you?"

"Hi, Dale, this Deputy Monroe."

"Well, hi there, Arness."

"You haven't by any chance gotten a call from Jackson, have you?"

"No. Should I?"

"I just came across his mail truck, but he isn't anywhere to be found. Thought he might have had engine trouble and called you."

"Nope, never called here. Hey, if you see him, tell him I'm still waiting on that shipment of oil filters that should have been here by now."

"Will do. Talk to you later, bye."

Deputy Monroe thought he should take a look around. Maybe Jackson had fallen down, had a heart attack, and was lying in the bushes.

He'd make a complete sweep of the area just to be sure.

But before he started looking for Jackson, he thought he would check his YouTube account on his cell phone and see how many hits he'd recently received of his new puppy playing with a neighbor's kitten that had gone viral with over a million hits so far.

He had just signed onto his account when he heard something scratching at the dirt behind the oak tree. He walked over and peered around the massive trunk.

The sound was giant centipedes, scampering out of a huge hole in the ground.

Deputy Monroe backed up and drew his service revolver.

A few of the creatures had shredded pieces of blue fabric caught in their pinchers.

He quickly realized the strips of material were from Jackson Tucker's uniform.

More centipedes clambered out of the ground, their shells covered in visceral gore and blood.

The deputy raised his cell phone so he could video the strange phenomenon.

Arness fired his gun at the creatures, capturing the action on his cell phone as he backed up to his car. He edged around the door. He cursed himself when he glanced inside for not closing the door when he first got out.

The centipedes were on him before he could get off another shot.

He flailed his arms to fight off the creatures, but there were too many. He dropped his cell phone on the car seat as the carnage and his demise were being uploaded worldwide on YouTube.

Deputy Arness Monroe was about to become the next viral sensation.

CHAPTER THIRTY-FIVE

"Before I pick up the dogs' order, would you be up for some food?"

"Sure," Frank replied.

Wanda swung the Chevy past the feed store and into a short alley, parking beside the Log Jam Diner.

They got out of the car and walked around to the front of the building. Frank held the door open.

Wanda gave him a strange look.

"What?" he asked.

"I don't know. It's been a while since anyone's held a door open for me."

"Contrary to popular belief, chivalry isn't dead."

Wanda smiled and stepped through the doorway. Frank closed the door behind him.

Peggy was waiting for them at the cash register. "Well, hi, Wanda."

"Thought we'd drop in for a quick bite."

"Table or counter?"

Wanda glanced at Frank.

"I don't care, counter's fine."

Wanda and Frank made themselves comfortable on the stools while Peggy brought their menus.

"Coffee?" she asked.

"Yes, please," Wanda said.

"I'd love some," Frank told the waitress.

"Peggy, this is Frank Travis. He's staying with us for a while."

"Nice to meet you, Peggy," Frank said.

"Pleasure is all mine."

Peggy poured them each a cup.

After a quick peek at the menu, Wanda said, "I'll have the chicken club, no fries."

"A BLT for me, and I'll have her fries," Frank said, giving Peggy a wink.

"Coming right up."

"Ever wonder where they came up with BLT?" Frank asked Wanda.

She gave him a look like he was an ignoramus.

"Gee, I don't know…bacon, lettuce, and tomato."

"Don't you think it should be called BLTB?"

"What in God's name for?"

"Well, you do put the BLT in between two slices of bread."

"Never thought of that before."

"I like to analyze things. Let's discuss that chicken in your club sandwich."

"What about it?"

"Chances are that chicken's pumped full of sodium."

"I'll take my chances."

Peggy brought over their plates and set them down on the counter.

"Looks good," Wanda said, gazing down at her sandwich.

Frank smiled and popped a french fry into his mouth.

***

"That hit the spot," Frank said as they came out of the diner.

"I'm going to get the car and park over at the feed store," Wanda said.

"All right. I need to walk off a few pounds. I'll meet you over there."

Wanda strolled around the corner and into the alley.

Frank checked both ways before he crossed the street which was being overly cautious, as they hadn't seen one car pass by the diner in the time it had taken them to eat their meal.

He could hear the Chevy's engine fire up across the street.

Frank thought he would wait for Wanda at the main entrance, but then he saw the portable toilet at the rear of the feed store. While they were dining, he had gotten up midway through his meal to use the restroom only to discover that it was out of order.

Peggy had explained that they were having plumbing problems and apologized for the inconvenience.

Frank glanced over his shoulder. Wanda hadn't backed out yet, so he decided this was the perfect opportunity to make a quick pit stop.

He walked down the side of the building toward the portable toilet, but as he got closer, he noticed a strange pool on the ground in front of the door.

It was blood.

Warily, he approached, listening for any telltale sound that might alert him to any danger or what might be lurking inside.

He reached for the door handle.

Something thumped against the interior wall.

"Jesus," Frank said, jumping back. He heard the Chevy pull into the dirt parking lot. He looked over and waved for Wanda to join him.

She got out of the car and strode over.

"What is it?" she asked.

"Look," Frank said, and pointed at the blood on the ground. "There's something moving around in there."

Wanda drew her nine-millimeter pistol from the holster.

"When I count to three, I want you to open the door and stand back. Understand?"

"Completely."

"One…"

Frank grabbed the handle.

"Two…"

He braced himself.

"Three!"

Frank yanked the door open.

Harmon Blackstone was sitting upright on the toilet seat. His pants were pulled down around his ankles. His shirt, underpants, bunched trousers, and boots were all slathered with his blood. A puddle had formed on the floor, spilling out under the door.

"Jesus," Frank said. "How long has he been in here?"

"I just saw him not too long ago."

"Well, it looks like rigor mortis has already set in."

"I don't know. This blood looks fresh."

"Then what's holding him up?"

Then, as if to answer Frank's question, a hard-shelled head bore out of Harmon's stomach. The engorged centipede was struggling to pull itself out.

Wanda wanted to shoot it, but that would mean firing into Harmon, and that didn't seem right, even though he was already dead.

Finally, the thing was far enough out that she could shot it without hitting Harmon.

"You son of a bitch," Wanda swore, and fired a rapid succession of bullets into the thing. The high-caliber slugs ripped the centipede to shreds.

No longer anchored down, Harmon keeled over and tumbled out of the portable toilet.

"Jesus, what a terrible way to go," Frank said.

Wanda glanced over at the feed store.

"Oh my God. Maxine!"

They ran around to the front of the building and entered the main entrance.

"Maxine! Can you hear me?" Wanda called out.

Frank searched around the store. "She's not here."

"Must be in the back."

Wanda held her pistol at the ready as they went behind the counter. She waited before stepping into the adjacent house. "Maxine? Are you in here?"

There was no reply.

Frank spotted a broom leaning against the wall. He grabbed it and snapped off the bristles, making it into a spear.

"It sure is dark in there." Wanda entered the small room that the Blackstone's used for storage.

She took a step and scanned the living room with the muzzle of her gun.

"The room looks clear."

"You never know. They could be anywhere," Frank whispered.

"Let's try the bedroom."

They headed down the narrow hallway.

Once they reached the bedroom door, Wanda felt along the wall for the light switch. "Found it."

The overhead light came on.

"Holy shit!" Frank said.

Maxine was lying on the bed, flat on her back. A centipede was coiled around her leg like a tourniquet, cutting off the circulation. Another centipede had wrapped itself around the woman's face and head forming a hard-shelled turban.

Frank stabbed the one on Maxine's leg, and ripped down its body. The centipede uncoiled and lay dead on the sheet.

He worked the tip of the broken-off broom handle under the other centipede clamped around Maxine's head and shoved the shaft through the creature, killing it.

"I've known Harmon and Maxine since I was a little girl." Wanda turned and her legs almost gave out.

Frank grabbed her before she went down. "Come on, let's go outside and get you some air."

***

Bron Kepler and Hondo were parked across the road from the Arco service station and had a good view of the goings-on in the feed store parking lot. They stayed slumped in their seats, so if anyone should glance up the road and see the Dodge truck, they might think it was unoccupied.

For over an hour, emergency vehicles had been funneling in and out of the parking area.

Kepler recognized Frank Travis standing next to a distraught woman wearing a uniformed shirt and a gun belt, leaning up against the front fender of a car.

"So Raymond Trodderman's protégé is here. And that must be Sheriff Wanda Rafferty," Kepler muttered to himself.

Hondo wasn't listening to Kepler's banter. He was too busy skinning a small garter snake.

Kepler looked over. "Must you, that thing stinks."

Hondo glanced up and smiled. His teeth looked like tiny Chiclets.

Kepler turned and gazed over at the feed store.

The entomologist was helping the sheriff into the passenger side of the car. He walked around the front, climbed in the driver's seat, and drove off down the road.

Kepler started up the truck. He followed the other car, keeping a fair distance between them so as not to be detected.

CHAPTER THIRTY-SIX

Donny looked down at his cell phone, and went onto the app for the Port of Oakland, displaying the schedules for the cargo gates. He picked the one with the least traffic, which was still congested, Oakland being the fifth busiest port in the United States.

After spending forty minutes in a long line behind the other freight carriers, Donny was finally allowed to pass through the gate. He had been given directions to where he was supposed to deliver his cargo.

He had never seen such a big operation. There were over a thousand twenty-foot-long intermodal cargo containers lined up in numerous rows stretching the length of an airport landing field.

Donny slowed down when he saw a dockworker, wearing a hardhat and a yellow vest, directing him to a loading bay. He pulled his rig around and backed up to the dock.

He shut down the engine and climbed down from the cab. He walked the length of the trailer and went up the steps to the loading dock. He unlocked the back of the trailer and opened the doors. Stepping inside, he pulled out his pallet jack.

A dockworker drove up in a forklift with an enclosed cab. He entered the rear of the trailer and scooped up the first pallet stacked six feet high with feed sacks.

Donny stood by and watched, leaning on the upright handle of his pallet jack.

The forklift driver carried the pallet across the dock and drove into a blue shipping container with International Organization for Standardization markings on the doors, along with the container number 345 in large white stencil.

The driver lowered the forks and placed the pallet on the floor of the forty-foot-long container then backed out and returned to get another pallet from the trailer.

Donny could see the towering Super Post-Panamax container cranes. The 22 behemoth cranes were the largest in the world and were as tall as a 25-story building.

He had heard long ago that the famous director George Lucas had gotten his idea for the AT-AT Walkers used in his *Star Wars* movies when he looked down and saw similar cargo cranes while flying into Oakland International Airport. Whether it was true or not, he wasn't sure, but the cranes were impressive.

Donny stared over at one of the container ships. The vessel was a quarter-mile long and almost two hundred feet tall above the waterline. The name *Far Horizon* was written on the side of the bow.

Longshoremen were busily working on the wharf. He watched a worker operating a giant lift drive up to the side of a twenty-foot container, pick it up, and maneuver under a huge crane.

Donny stopped a dockworker walking by.

"How many containers can a ship like that carry?"

The dockworker looked up at the humongous cargo vessel. "That one, maybe ten thousand."

"They can stack that many on the deck?"

"They don't have decks. Container ships are basically empty hulls. Those containers you see above the ship's hull are only the tip of the iceberg of what's down below."

"That's some load."

"Once her cargo bay is filled, you're looking at somewhere over 300,000 tons."

"You've got to be kidding."

"I know, it's a wonder they even float," the dockworker said, and walked off.

A short time later, the forklift driver loaded the last pallet into the blue cargo container and shut off the machine.

He got out of the enclosed cab, walked up to the open doors of the container, and closed them.

Donny pushed his pallet jack back inside the empty trailer and strapped it down so that it wouldn't roll around while he was driving. He closed the rear doors.

A dockworker signed off on the paperwork and handed it back to Donny.

He walked around the side of the trailer and climbed up in the cab. "Holiday Inn, here I come."

CHAPTER THIRTY-SEVEN

Wanda was on her second cup of coffee and was feeling more herself.

"That was pretty rough," Frank said, sitting across from her at the kitchen table.

"I'll be okay," she told him. "I have a question."

"What's that?"

"Back when we were trapped in the Jeep—"

"You mean, when I got bitten and I didn't die?"

"Well, yeah." Wanda shook her head. "I'm sorry, that sounded kind of weird."

"No, not at all. The doctor wondered the same thing. After I told him how many times I'd been bitten and stung through the years, he figured my body had built up a tolerance."

Dillon walked into the kitchen having overheard Frank and his mother's last exchange and said, "Does that mean you're a superhero?"

Frank looked down at the small boy. "Hardly, but it is a good reminder that I should be more careful handling insects. Remember what I told you."

"Wear gloves."

"That's right."

Wanda glanced over at the phone on the counter. She got up and walked over to check the answering machine. There were no messages.

"I would have thought Special Agent Grover would have gotten back to us by now."

"Maybe he has other cases he's working on."

Ally rushed into the kitchen. "Mom, you've got to see this!" She handed her cell phone to her mother.

Wanda looked at the screen. A video was playing, but it was difficult to understand what was happening, as the images were blurry because things kept darting in front of the camera lens.

The shot went to another angle, and Wanda saw her deputy's face.

"Oh my God, that's Arness."

The man screamed as half a dozen giant centipedes piled on top of him and began ripping at his flesh.

"Where'd you get this?" Wanda asked Ally.

"On YouTube. Everyone's watching it. It's only been up for thirty minutes, and it's already got over fifty thousand hits."

The phone rang on the kitchen counter.

"That must be Grover," Frank said.

Wanda ran for the phone and picked it up. "Hello?"

She listened for a moment. "Yes, I know where that is. We'll be right there."

Frank got up from the table. "Was that him?"

"No," Wanda said. "That was the Forestry Service. They got an emergency dispatch saying that there are hikers up on the mountain that need assistance. They're holding a chopper for us."

"But why call you?"

"He said they sounded crazy. Like maybe they were on drugs and it might be a good idea if there was law enforcement present."

"What were they saying?"

"That they'd found a cave full of giant insects."

***

The Bell 204 hovered over the flat granite wide enough for a helipad and touched down. Wanda and Frank kept their heads low as they stepped out of the whirlybird and onto the ground.

A young couple was standing fifty feet away, waving their arms.

Wanda and Frank rushed over.

"I'm Sheriff Rafferty, and this is Frank Travis," Wanda said, making introductions.

"Jake Carver. This is my wife, Nora."

"Thank God you're here," Nora said.

"Are either of you hurt?' Wanda asked.

"I've been shot," Jake told the sheriff.

"Shot? By who?"

"Craig Porter."

"Someone you know?"

"Craig and his wife, Gail, came up here with us. Gail was attacked by one of those centipedes. She's dead."

"And where's Craig?"

"He's dead as well," Jake said. "I swear I was only defending myself."

Wanda looked at the hatchet in Jake's hand. There was blood on the blade.

"You better give me that."

Jake handed her the hatchet.

Wanda pulled out a large evidence bag out of her back pocket and slipped the hatchet inside.

"Where are their bodies?"

"Gail's up on the ridge. Craig's down by the trail."

"Let me tell the pilot to shut down while we go check. Jake, come with me and wait in the chopper." Wanda walked over to the helicopter and opened the passenger door for Jake.

"This man needs medical attention. Afterward, we can get him to a hospital," Wanda told the pilot.

"Step in and I'll check you over," the pilot said to Jake.

"There are two other hikers, but I was told they were dead. We're going to take a look. Shouldn't be more than half an hour."

As Wanda walked back to Frank and Nora, the pilot switched off the turbo engine, which gradually whined down.

"Show us where the bodies are," Wanda said to Nora.

After hiking up the steep ledge that led to the top of the ridge, they came across Gail's body lying in the midst of the disheveled campsite.

"Oh, my God," Nora said. "What's happened to her?"

"How long has she been dead?" Wanda asked.

"A day," Nora replied. "Surely, she couldn't have decomposed this fast."

Frank knelt to get a closer look at the rotted corpse. The flesh on the woman's face had partially sloughed off her skull like her head had been steamed in a slow pressure cooker.

"Let's take a look at her husband," Wanda said.

The three went back down the narrow ledge and trudged past the lakes to the path that led to the fork in the trail.

They found Craig's body at the trail marker, his gun by his side.

Wanda used her pen, picked the weapon up by the trigger guard, and slipped it inside of another evidence bag.

"So why did Craig shoot your husband?" Wanda asked.

"I don't know. He just flipped out. We were arguing, and before we knew it, he pulled out his gun. Please don't arrest us. Craig even tried to kill me. Pushed me down a shaft and left me there to die. I was trying to find a way out when I happened on those creatures. You do believe me, don't you?"

"Yes, we believe you," Wanda told her. "We've seen them, too."

"You said they were in a cave," Frank said.

"Yes, there has to be hundreds of them."

"How big would you say?"

"They vary, but I saw some as long as twenty feet."

"That would be the Maximus," Frank said. "What else can you tell us?"

"I think they're breeding. I saw eggs. And some were fighting, even eating each other."

"That's not good."

"Why, what is it?" Wanda asked.

"By feeding on one another, they become more venomous. An untreated bite can become gangrenous in no time, much like a flesh-eating disease." Frank looked at Nora. "That explains the rapid decomposition of your friend."

"Do you remember where the entrance to the cave is?"

"Yes, I could take you there."

"No," Wanda said. "First, we need to get you and Jake to a hospital."

"What then?" Frank asked.

"We get the military involved. I'm sure someone in uniform has seen poor Arness's video by now."

CHAPTER THIRTY-EIGHT

The barn was Ryan's domain.

An old tractor and a rotary plow that hadn't been used for decades were rusting in the rear of the structure. Ryan kept pestering his mom to have the farm equipment hauled away, but she said she liked having them there for nostalgic reasons.

Ryan had converted the barn into a mechanics bay, and often worked on his friends' cars for some quick cash. Of course, Dale at the Arco wouldn't have been too pleased if he knew he had someone stealing his business, so Ryan told his friends not to broadcast that he was fixing their cars.

He had a fair amount of hand tools hanging on a pegboard wall. There were plenty of electrical sockets on his ten-foot-long workbench to plug in his power tools like his electric drills, saber saw, and circular saw. He also had a table saw next to the workbench for ripping boards and cutting lumber.

When he wasn't working on cars, he liked to dabble in carpentry, and thought after he graduated from high school that he would like to take up a trade and become a journeyman instead of going to college.

He'd spent countless hours on the '56 Chevy, getting the automobile in working order for his mom. He thought about restoring the car to classic status, but he didn't have the money to spend chrome plating everything under the hood and customizing the body with some cherry metal flake paint job.

He worked part-time after school at the hardware store, earning a meager paycheck which only paid for gas, car insurance, and upkeep for one car—and that was his '71 Pontiac Firebird Trans Am. His pride and joy.

Ryan leaned under the open hood, unscrewed the wing nut, and removed the cover on the air filter casing. He took out the dirty air filter and tossed it on the workbench. The housing was wiped out with a clean rag and a new air filter was put in. He replaced the lid and screwed the wing nut back on.

He went over to the workbench where some of his tools were laid out. He grabbed a socket wrench and went back to the car. Work mats covered the fenders so that he wouldn't scratch the paint while working on the engine.

One time, he had forgotten he'd left a screwdriver in his back pocket and had punctured the seat when he got in his car. That was the first, and last time, he ever did that again.

Leaning over the fender, he pulled the black rubber-insulated wires off of the four sparkplugs on the one side of the big block 455 cubic inch V8 engine. He used the socket wrench and unscrewed the four spark plugs. He went around to the other fender, unplugged those wires, and removed the other four spark plugs. The blackened plugs were left on the mat covering the right fender, as he wanted to clean them up and see if any of them could be salvaged.

Ryan had already taken the new spark plugs out of their packages, and after consulting his manual, had properly set the gap for each one.

He spent half an hour putting in the new spark plugs, and another fifteen minutes replacing the points in the distributor cap.

Ryan shoved his floor jack under the front brace of his car and pumped the handle. The front tires rose off the ground. He stopped when the Trans Am was high enough to crawl underneath so that he could unscrew the nut on the oil pan and drain the old oil.

As he often worked alone, he was always conscious of safety, and placed a jack stand under each side of the front end to prevent the car from slamming down on top of him in the event the floor jack should fail.

He kicked his creeper across the dirt and positioned it beside the car. He grabbed the appropriate socket wrench and a droplight that was plugged into the workbench. Scooting his upper body onto the creeper, he pushed himself under the car with the heels of his boots. A plastic oil catcher was under the pan.

Ryan was placing the socket over the drain plug when he heard something scrabbling across the dirt not too far away. He tilted his head back, viewing everything upside down, and saw a strange shape dart behind the front tire.

He could hear it clambering up the rubber tire and the chrome rim then up onto the protective mat.

Ryan shined the droplight up between the firewall and the engine mount and tried to get a good look, but the starter motor was blocking his view.

Objects started clattering, ricocheting off the metal engine, and hailing down on Ryan's head. One of the old spark plugs smacked him in the forehead, and would have struck his right eye if he hadn't moved his head out of the way in time.

Ryan grabbed the undercarriage of the car and pushed himself out from under the Trans Am. As soon as he was clear, he scrambled to his feet.

A three-foot-long centipede was climbing over the air filter casing and was crawling onto the fender mat.

Ryan reached up and slammed the hood down, severing the creature's head.

"Where in the hell did you come from?" He looked down at the decapitated head, still moving about in the dirt. He lifted his boot and squashed the thing.

He heard a noise behind him and turned.

"What the—?"

Another giant centipede was racing across the dirt.

Biology had never been one of Ryan's strongest subjects in school, so he had no idea if these creatures had eyes, or if they were blind and had to feel around with their antennae to search for prey.

He reached down, snagged the cord, and dragged the droplight out from under the car. When the centipede was close enough, he aimed the bright bulb in its direction.

The creature scurried back and darted under the Trans Am.

There was more scuttling in the shadows.

Ryan wondered if they were drawn to sound. He edged over to the table saw and switched on the machine. The circular blade spun, creating a high-pitched whine.

A centipede converged on one of the table saw's legs. The creature gripped the metal with its many powerful claws, and as it undulated its body, slowly shimmied up onto the flat surface.

Ryan grabbed a shovel that was leaning against the workbench. He swung the garden tool at the centipede, scooping it into the spinning blade. The razor sharp teeth ripped through its body, cutting it in half.

He heard something rattling behind him, and turned.

A centipede was climbing over the pegboard, bumping the hand tools off their hooks. A set of screwdrivers fell, then a ball-peen hammer.

The centipede clung to the pegboard and arched its back, showing Ryan its deadly fangs.

Ryan snatched up the hammer and struck the centipede, over and over until it finally went limp and fell onto the workbench.

He grabbed a cordless saber saw and a battery-operated drill with a six-inch drill bit off the workbench and turned them both on. The table saw and the hand-held tools reverberated, creating a deafening cacophony within the barn.

Ryan stood his ground like the cult film actor Bruce Campbell, portraying the manic Ash Williams in *The Evil Dead*, as he waited for another centipede to attack.

He was glancing over his shoulder to make sure that they weren't sneaking up on him when he spotted the perfect weapon.

CHAPTER THIRTY-NINE

Ally was tidying up her room when she heard the racket coming from the barn through her window. She recognized the distinct sound of the table saw and some other power tools. She wondered what in the world Ryan was working on that he needed all those tools going at once.

Ally walked out of her bedroom and went downstairs.

She thought she would peek in on Dillon.

At first glance, she didn't see him. As usual, his toys, comic books, and clothes looked like they had washed ashore into his bedroom. He'd propped open his window with a Hulk action figure. Rochelle was up on Dillon's bed, fast asleep, lying on her back with her legs in the air.

"Dillon? Where are you?"

She heard paper riffling and then a quick thump from behind the Yosemite Sam cardboard cutout standing in the corner of the room.

"Dillon, what are you doing?"

"Nothing," he said, crawling out from behind the three-foot-tall Looney Tunes character.

"I was going to make myself a sandwich. Want one?" Ally asked.

"If you cut the crust off."

"Better not let Mom see your room like this."

Dillon gave her a look that translated to: *You're not the boss of me.*

He walked over, looked up at Alley, and slowly shut his bedroom door in her face.

Ally stared at the closed door. "Don't you get an attitude, Mr. Smarty Pants."

"Okey dokey," he replied from the other side of the door.

Ally shook her head and walked across the living room into the kitchen.

Winston was lying on his side on the floor, and he wasn't moving. Something was sticking out of his neck.

Ally knelt on the floor.

"Where is it?"

Turing to the voice, Ally saw a man, wearing a fedora with a sweat-stained band and a coarse leather coat, standing on the other side of the kitchen table.

He had a gun, holstered on his belt.

"What did you do to our dog?"

"I didn't do anything."

Ally heard shuffling behind her. She looked over her shoulder and saw a strange little man with facial tattoos.

He held a blowgun a few inches from his mouth.

"I have only to give the word," the other man said.

"What do you want?"

"Trodderman's journal."

"I don't know what you're talking about. Who are you?"

"I'm Bron Kepler. My associate is Hondo. We mean you no harm. Just give me the journal."

Ally returned her attention to Winston. "You call this no harm?" She placed her hand on the dog's chest. She couldn't feel him breathing. She pulled the yellow-feathered dart out of the bull terrier's neck.

She glared at Kepler and said in a malignant tone, "You better not have killed our dog."

Dillon's bedroom door flew open and the boy ran out. "Okay, I'm done. Where's my sandwich?"

"Dillon! Get back in your room!" Ally yelled.

The boy stopped in the middle of the living room.

Hondo turned. He pointed his blowgun at Dillon and puffed up his cheeks.

Rochelle knocked Dillon aside as she barreled by and charged the man threatening her young master.

Hondo blew out the dart, which struck the hefty bulldog in the shoulder, but it didn't deter the burly powerhouse, determined to save Dillon from this evil man.

Kepler drew his pistol and pointed his weapon at the charging dog.

Ally grabbed the side of the kitchen table and shoved it at Kepler. He jumped back to avoid being struck, throwing off his aim.

Rochelle suddenly faltered and collapsed at the doorway to the kitchen as if the bones in her legs had instantly turned to jelly. She lay on her side with her tongue hanging out of her mouth.

"You killed my dog!" Dillon screamed.

Hondo placed another dart in his blowgun.

Ally was about to push past Hondo and snatch up Dillon when there was a loud bang in the mudroom.

Ryan threw open the backdoor. He burst into the kitchen and slammed the door shut.

He looked crazy like he was being pursued by a pack of wolves. He was brandishing a portable blowtorch with a push button igniter. His shirt was splattered with goop as if kids throwing balloons filled with lime-green paint had ambushed him.

"Keep the doors shut. The barn's infested with—" he yelled then stopped when he saw the two strange men standing in his kitchen.

"Who are these guys?" Ryan asked his sister.

"They're bad men."

"That so." Ryan considered Kepler, holding the gun. He looked over at Hondo, his blowgun near his lips.

Ryan gazed down and saw the two dogs lying on the floor.

"Son of a bitch," he said then glared at the two intruders. "You did this?"

"Just give us the journal, and we'll leave."

Ryan looked at Ally, but by the blank look on her face, he realized she was just as confused as he was.

Kepler took a step toward Ryan. "I will only ask—"

Ryan slammed the bottom of the portable blowtorch on Kepler's wrist.

Kepler yelped and dropped his gun.

Hondo turned to shoot Ryan with his blowgun, but before he could muster up a breath, Ally side kicked the Indian hard in the knee, dropping him to the floor.

"Run!" Ryan yelled.

Ally dashed into the living room. She scooped Dillon up in her arms and ran into the boy's bedroom.

Ryan was right behind as they rushed into the room. He quickly closed the door and locked it. "Quick," he said to Ally. "Help me with Dillon's dresser."

They got behind the piece of furniture and scooted it across the hardwood floor to block the door.

Dillon was crying, having just witnessed that creepy man hurt Rochelle.

"We need to call Mom," Ally said, putting a consoling arm around her little brother. "Do you have your cell phone?" she asked Ryan.

"No, I left it in the barn. You?"

"Upstairs, in my room."

"Then we're screwed."

CHAPTER FORTY

"I've seen that truck before," Wanda said, drawing Frank's attention to the Dodge pickup parked a hundred yards down from her farmhouse, as she pulled the Chevy onto the gravel driveway. "It was across from the Arco station."

"You don't think it could be Kepler?"

"We better make sure the kids are okay," Wanda said, and jumped out of the car.

They rushed around to the back of the house.

Wanda quietly opened the mudroom door and they stepped inside. Normally, whenever she answered a call where she thought she was walking into danger, she would draw her gun; but this was her house and her children were inside, so she decided to keep her Browning semi-automatic holstered.

She approached the backdoor leading into the kitchen. She looked through the windowpane.

"I don't see anyone. Wait…oh no."

"What is it?" Frank said, and peered through the glass.

Wanda opened the door slowly.

She stepped into the kitchen and saw the still dogs, lying on the floor.

Frank went over and knelt beside Rochelle. He plucked the dart out of her shoulder and sniffed the tip.

He placed two fingers on the dog's inner thigh, feeling for a pulse. He looked up at Wanda. "She's still alive."

"Check Winston." Wanda walked around Frank as he scooted across the floor to examine the bull terrier. She stepped into the living room.

"Ally? Ryan?" she called out.

"We're in here," Ally yelled from Dillon's room.

Wanda was halfway across the living room when a man suddenly appeared, pointing a pistol at her.

She instinctually reached for her sidearm but knew he had the drop on her and moved her hand slowly away from her holster. She held her arms up in front of her chest to show him that she wasn't going for her gun.

"Where is it?" he asked.

Frank walked into the room. "I think Winston…" and then he stopped speaking when he saw Bron Kepler pointing his gun at Wanda.

"All right Travis. Give me the journal."

"I don't think so."

"Then, I'm afraid, you leave me no choice."

Wanda caught movement out of the corner of her eye and turned as a brown-skinned man popped up from behind the couch. He had a blowgun pressed to his lips. He puffed up his cheeks, and blew out a dart.

Frank jumped in front of Wanda.

The yellow-feathered dart struck Frank in the neck. He reached up and pulled it out.

"Hondo, you son of a…" Frank muttered, marching toward the Indian.

Hondo inserted another similarly-tipped dart and puffed on his blowgun.

This time, Frank was slower to yank the dart out as he stumbled forward.

"Just kill him," Kepler yelled at the Indian.

Hondo reached inside his pouch and pulled out a red-feathered dart.

With all eyes on Hondo, Wanda drew her Browning and fired twice.

Kepler flew back against the wall.

She turned and shot Hondo. The bullet punctured the Indian's throat, and when he gasped, he inhaled the deadly dart. He collapsed behind the couch.

Once she was certain the two men were dead, she went over to Frank, who was down on one knee in a determining effort not to fall.

"You're one tough hombre, Frank Travis."

"Glad you think so," he smiled, woozily. "You better make sure your kids are okay."

Wanda walked over to the bedroom door. "You can come out now."

She could hear something being dragged across the hardwood floor on the other side of the door.

Ally screamed, and then Ryan shouted, "Jesus, they're coming in through the window."

Wanda pounded on the door. "What's going on? Open the door!"

She heard the doorknob rattle.

She pushed and the door opened enough that she could stick her head through. Dillon's dresser was blocking the door. She could smell smoke.

Ryan had a portable blowtorch, and was setting something on fire as it crawled through the window and onto the floor. She saw a giant centipede clamber over the windowsill from the outside, and realized that the creatures were invading the house.

Her son turned his torch on the new intruder, and it too, was engulfed in flames but instead of withering and dying, the creature scampered down into the room, igniting clothes and books on the floor.

The curtains were already ablaze.

Yosemite Sam was engulfed in flames as the fire crept up the wall, burning posters of Batman, and a group shot of the Justice League.

Wanda pushed with all her might and shoved the dresser back.

"Get out of there!" she yelled.

Ally picked up Dillon and headed for the door while Ryan knocked the Hulk figurine out from under the wood frame and slammed the window down. The room was thick with smoke.

Once Ally and Dillon had slipped out between the dresser and the door, Wanda rushed into the kitchen. She opened the pantry and grabbed the fire extinguisher. She raced back to Dillon's room.

"Ryan." She handed her son the canister. He pulled the pin and immediately started blasting the room with fire retardant. A white cloud gradually replaced the black smoke as the foam smothered the flames.

Ally hugged her little brother as they watched Ryan put the last small fire out. "See, Dillon? This is what happens when you don't clean up your room."

Frank stumbled over and leaned against the doorjamb. "Everyone okay?"

"Yeah, I think so," Wanda said.

Ryan was kicking things on the floor to make sure there weren't any smoldering embers.

He looked across the room. "Sorry, Dillon, but it looks like Yosemite Sam is a goner." The cardboard cutout was blackened and unrecognizable. "What's this?" He bent down and picked up what looked like the charred remains of an incinerated telephone book.

Wanda looked at her son. "Dillon, you didn't take…"

"But I wanted to see the pictures," he said in his defense.

"So much for Raymond's journal," Frank groaned.

CHAPTER FORTY-ONE

A CH-47 Chinook military transport helicopter descended and landed on the granite plain. The side door opened and fifty soldiers filed out. The troops quickly formed into two platoons.

Ten men were armed with flamethrowers with twin tanks strapped on their backs, one tank holding the flammable liquid, the other the pressurized gas to propel the flame.

The other soldiers carried assault rifles and combat shotguns. Each man had hand grenades clipped to the front of his jacket.

A colonel, wearing a similar camouflage uniform as his men, and sporting two pearl-handled forty-fives on his webbed belt, stepped out of the aircraft, followed by Frank, Wanda, and Nora. Wanda carried her Remington pump shotgun under the crook of her arm.

"If at all possible, I would like to get a live specimen," Frank said to the colonel.

"How dangerous did you say these things are?" the military commander asked.

Frank hesitated for a moment. "They're extremely deadly."

"Then, I don't see as we have any other choice but to eradicate the miserable sons-of-bitches."

The colonel approached his men.

"Everyone, listen up. You all have your orders and know what to do. This is a simple op. We go in and fry the little bastards. Once we're back at the base, every man here is getting a special three-day pass."

The short speech rallied up the troops and they cheered.

The colonel turned to Nora. "All right, young lady, if you would kindly take point and show us the way."

Nora headed toward the trail that led down the mountainside. Wanda and Frank walked behind the colonel. Some of the soldiers followed in single file while a small number split from the main group and fanned out to take up predetermined tactical positions.

After a twenty-minute hike, Nora pointed to the entrance to the cave.

The colonel turned to his men. "Flamethrowers, you go in first. Once you find their den, light 'em up. Burn 'em to a crisp. After the smoke clears, we find any stragglers, squash the mothers."

He pointed to the men that were to be the first wave. "Give 'em hell, boys."

A small band of soldiers entered the mouth of the cave.

They followed the tunnel that stretched inside the mountain and soon reached the antechamber. Everywhere was crawling with enormous centipedes.

Three soldiers stood shoulder-to-shoulder with their flamethrowers and aimed the muzzles of their gun housings. "Flame on," one of the men shouted, mimicking Johnny Storm, the Human Torch of the *Fantastic Four*.

Short bursts of flammable liquid shot out of their guns stretching more than twenty feet. The men shut off their equipment to assess the damage.

The ground was a frenzy of burning creatures, squirming and climbing over one another, some unscathed only to be set on fire by those already in flames.

"Again!"

Three more long jets of yellow fire scorched the cavern floor.

The soldiers levered the feed pipes, having depleted their fuel tanks.

"Second wave," one of them shouted.

The soldiers backed toward the tunnel to make room for their replacements already entering the cavern.

A centipede scurried up the pant leg of a soldier. Another creature dropped from the ceiling onto a soldier's shoulder, wrapping its body around his neck.

"Watch out," a man screamed when he saw a three-foot-long centipede latch onto a fellow soldier's chest and bite into his face.

One of the flamethrower replacements was adjusting his gun when a centipede came up behind, crawled up his leg onto his back, and savagely drove its fangs into the man's neck.

The soldier jerked back his hand, accidentally switching on his flamethrower as he fell in a twisted heap.

Liquid fire spewed out the end of his gun and swept over the other soldiers, setting them on fire.

***

Wanda could hear the horrific screams echoing deep in the cave. "Sounds like they're in trouble," she said to Frank.

"Hope the colonel didn't underestimate them."

A soldier ran out of the cave. He tore off his helmet and staggered across the rocks. The skin on his face looked like gray poi. He took a few more steps and collapsed.

Twenty-some centipedes charged out of the cave and attacked the soldiers.

Every man laid down a steady barrage of gunfire. The bullets ripped through the creatures, some of the projectiles ricocheting off the stone ground and rocks.

"Get down," Wanda said, as she grabbed Nora and pulled her to the ground. Frank dove down as well.

One soldier was struck in the face and dropped to the ground.

A giant centipede came at Wanda. She waited until it was five feet away and blew it to pieces with her shotgun.

She looked up and saw a soldier walking across the rocks, firing his machinegun back and forth on the ground like he was hosing down a deck with a power washer.

Wanda, Frank, and Nora stood just as a gigantic centipede emerged out of the cave. The twenty-foot long creature was blackened from being burned, some of its rear legs still on fire. It hobbled across the rock, seemingly in pain.

"That's the one that shed its skin," Nora said.

Wanda ratcheted her shotgun.

"My God, it's incredible!" Frank was so struck by its magnificence that he could only watch in awe.

The soldiers were less impressed. Ten of them surrounded the smoldering abomination. They opened fire and the centipede immediately coiled up to protect itself only to become a better target. The bullets ripped into the soft flesh. Green goop spurted out of its body.

Some of the soldiers paused to reload while the others kept firing, the din from the rifles and machineguns so deafening that no one heard the second Maximus exiting the cave.

Racing across the granite, the enormous creature attacked the circle of men. It whipped its body, knocking three soldiers flat on the ground, and then stamped its pointy legs like impaling spears into their bodies. One soldier's head was caught in a vise-like grip and crushed between the powerful pinchers.

The Maximus dove onto another man and injected him with its deadly venom. A soldier fired his rifle but the bullets glanced off the monster's hard shell.

"Frank, what do we do?" Wanda yelled. She punched his shoulder to break him out of his rapture.

"What?"

"How do we kill it?"

"There's only one way," Frank said. He turned to a small cluster of soldiers that were warily approaching the centipede annihilating their comrades. "Use your grenades! Roll them underneath the underbelly!"

The men unhooked their grenades from their vests and pitched the bombs.

Everyone ducked for cover.

A dozen grenades went off split seconds from one another, the blasts so great, they collectively lifted the humongous centipede off the ground as the shrapnel tore it apart. Huge armored chunks rained down on the rocks.

The colonel yelled, "Seal it up!"

Three soldiers ran up to the mouth of the cave. They unclipped grenades from their vests, pulled the pins, and lobbed the small bombs as far back as they could.

Shortly after, a series of loud explosions erupted inside the tunnel. Dust and smoke belched out, followed by the sound of crumbling rock.

Once, the dust settled, the cave-in had blocked off the entrance.

There were only a few of the smaller centipedes still alive, scrambling for somewhere to hide, but the soldiers were picking them off, one by one.

Wanda looked around and counted only fifteen soldiers remaining, including the colonel.

Frank stared at the rocks sealing up the cave. "I guess that's the end of that."

"There's still another way out," Nora said, unable to conceal the worried look on her face.

***

The centipedes that had survived the inferno scurried up the ledge that overlooked the grotto and squirmed into the narrow tunnel. They followed the fissure, racing in the darkness, thousands of tiny clawed-legs clicking along the stone.

Soon, they reached the shaft, piling up in an anthropoid traffic jam, some of them sliding down onto the backpacks at the bottom of the pit.

With their sharp claws, they dug into the stone and began to scale the sheer walls.

Some of them were actually almost to the rim when the two soldiers above blasted the shaft with their flamethrowers.

CHAPTER FORTY-TWO

Hugh Brown climbed up the steel steps of the Hyster loaded container handler and opened the door to the cab. He sat in the contoured seat behind the steering wheel, reached over, and closed the door. Before he started the engine, he wiped his hand down over his face. He was so hungover from staying out late drinking with his buddies the previous night that he had been tempted to call in sick.

But that would have been the last straw. He was already on probation. His supervisor had warned him that if he failed to report for work or had the slightest infraction while performing his duties, Brown would be seeking employment elsewhere.

So he had no choice but to report for work, even though Sharon Stone was stabbing an ice pick in the back of his skull. He dug three packets of aspirin out of his coat pocket, and after opening them, popped the tablets in his mouth. He worked up enough spit and swallowed.

He started the Cummings diesel engine and turned on the air conditioning. The cool air coming out of the vents gave him some marginal relief. He engaged the powershift transmission and drove across the yard.

The container ship *Far Horizon* loomed high above the dock. The vessel was a few containers shy of being fully loaded. Five forty-footers were waiting to be hoisted onboard and placed on top of the other containers in a space in front of the ship's bridge.

Brown jockeyed the large loader over to a blue cargo container—number 345—that was fifty feet away from the other containers.

He gripped the joystick and positioned the hydraulic spreader over the top of the metal container and lowered it down engaging the twist locks. He raised the mast and picked up the container.

He cupped the suicide knob in his hand, spun the steering wheel, and gunned the Hyster loader across the tarmac toward the other five containers.

Coming alongside one of the containers, Brown lowered the blue sea van.

He heard the grinding of metal on metal, and a clank on the cement.

"Shit!" he swore. He left the engine idling, got out of the cab, and raced down the steps.

He went over and looked between the two containers. He'd come in too close when bringing down the blue container and sheered off the padlock along with the long rod that kept one of the doors closed.

Brown glanced around to see if anyone was watching. He didn't see any other longshoremen nearby that might have witnessed his screw up. He looked straight up but couldn't see the crane operator, which meant the man, couldn't see him.

He had only seconds to fix this. He raced back to the Hyster and up the steps to the cab. A toolbox was on the floor. He opened the lid, found a coil of baling wire and a pair of wire cutters.

Brown clambered down the steps and rushed over to the blue container. He pushed the one door closed, and looped the wire through the eyelet meant for the padlock, and cut off the excess.

He tested the door. It wasn't firmly sealed, but it would have to do.

He grabbed the broken padlock and the metal pole off the ground and carried them back to the Hyster.

Brown unhooked the container and backed up. He cranked the wheel and drove off, searching for the nearest dumpster.

CHAPTER FORTY-THREE

Wanda and Frank sat on the front porch at the top of the steps, gazing at the field across the road. The sky was darkening, and the clouds were turning a brilliant flamingo-pink from the setting sun.

"I love sitting out here in the evening," Wanda said.

"It is nice. Oh, did I tell you? I may have a position at UC Davis."

"Really. Does that mean you're sticking around?"

"Looks that way," Frank smiled and hoisted his beer.

Wanda smiled back and clinked her bottled beer against Frank's.

"Seems they want an entomologist with some field experience. Someone that can captivate the students."

"Sounds right up your alley."

"Yeah, I guess I have a few tales I could share."

Ally was completing a jog and came running up.

Frank and Wanda moved apart and made room for Ally to get past.

"How was your run?" Wanda asked.

"I set myself a new personal best," Ally replied.

"Good for you."

"I'm going to take a shower."

"Dinner in an hour," Wanda said as her daughter opened the front screen door and went into the house as Ryan was coming out. He stood on the porch, wiping his hands with a rag, paint flecks on his face and hair.

"I've finished with Dillon's room. Can you tell him to keep his grubby little hands off the walls?"

"I'll do my best," Wanda replied.

Ryan held the screen door open for Winston and Rochelle. The two dogs sauntered out and lay by the railing near Wanda. Ryan went back inside.

"Looks like they're recovering just fine. They were lucky that damn Indian didn't use his poison-tipped darts," Frank commented.

"Like he was going to use on you?"

"Yeah."

Dillon walked around the side of the house and stopped at the foot of the steps. He was holding a large Mason jar with a pair of Ryan's work gloves.

"What do you have there?" Wanda asked.

"A tarantula. Want to see it?"

"No, take that away."

"Let me take a look." Frank got up and went down the steps.

Dillon handed Frank the jar.

"I see you're wearing gloves. That's good," Frank said, approvingly.

"Just like you told me," Dillon replied. "So what's the big word for this one?"

"Well, the scientific name for tarantulas is *Aphonepelma*. This one is your common variety and harmless. By the looks of her, I'd say she's pregnant. Must be their mating season."

"Are you serious, that thing's pregnant?" Wanda said, standing and backing onto the porch.

"Did you hear that, Mom, she's going to have babies," Dillon said, proudly.

"You better not bring that in the house," Wanda warned.

"Come on, let's take her into the field and let her go," Frank said to Dillon.

"Okey dokey."

Wanda waited until they were halfway across the road until she finally sat back down on the porch. She watched Frank and Dillon walk out onto the field, searching for the perfect spot to release the tarantula.

It would be nice having Frank around, she thought to herself, smiling, as she took a sip of her beer.

CHAPTER FORTY-FOUR

Jeremiah Freeman had the best job in the world.

Many of his friends disagreed and kept insisting he change his profession, that what he did for a living was too dangerous. His wife often worried and said she knew how police officers' wives felt whenever they watched their husbands go off to work every day, praying they would return home safely.

His brother-in-law was always after him to go work at Google where business was booming, but Jeremiah always declined and said he couldn't see himself confined to a cubicle all day. He might as well be a prisoner locked up in a cell.

Jeremiah was the outdoors type. He'd worked construction when he was younger before he became a house painter. He was good at what he did and always took pride in his work.

His work ethic and his fearless commitment later earned him a position as a painter working on one of the most iconic structures in the world—the Golden Gate Bridge.

Jeremiah always thought of the structure as the Eighth Wonder of the World.

He was one of a few elite squads of men that risked their lives everyday, making sure the international orange suspension bridge was preserved and guarded against the corrosive salt air and the damaging moisture threatening to turn it into a rust bucket.

An estimated 40 million cars traveled over the bridge each year. Jeremiah wasn't surprised as he'd seen the commuter traffic in the mornings and afternoons. One thing he learned early on was not to look down at the cars driving below, as it always gave him vertigo. The same feeling came over him whenever he was on one of the suspension cables and happened to look down at the current passing under the bridge.

Last thing he wanted was to get dizzy, especially when he was on top of one of the tower spires, seven hundred feet above the waters of San Francisco Bay.

There had been a number of people that had committed suicide, jumping off the bridge. He'd read that it only took four seconds to plummet 245 feet to the water. By then, the person was traveling over 75 miles an hour during impact, and in most cases, died instantly.

One of Jeremiah's coworkers had witnessed someone standing on the railing about to jump, and even tried to coax the man down, but he'd been too distraught and jumped anyway. Watching that man fall still haunted the fellow painter, even to this day.

Jeremiah hoped never to see anything as horrific.

Today, he and a squad of other painters were tasked with coating rivets, which was a year-round job, as there were over a million rivets holding the bridge together.

He put on his harness belt and fastened his self-retracting lifelines to the safety wires. He carried a pail of thick paint and a broad-bristled paintbrush attached to a long handle, and started up the yard-wide cable.

The fog was clearing. By the time the pail was empty, he would be standing high enough to see all of San Francisco, Marin, Oakland, and the South Bay.

It really was the best job in the world.

***

The *Far Horizon* got underway and pulled out of the Port of Oakland. The cargo container ship, operated by only a 13-man crew, cruised up the narrow estuary and entered the San Francisco Bay.

Inside the bridge, the captain was plotting a course on a large chart, and consulting an array of computers. The chief officer went about the complex control room, conducting a systems check off of the ship's radar and navigation. He passed by the gyrocompass and noted the heading.

He gazed out through a glass pane of the wraparound windshield. He could see the Golden Gate Bridge over the bow, stretched over the channel. Alcatraz Island was just off the starboard side.

A crewmember was standing out on the observation deck. He was leaning over the railing and looking down. He turned, went around the foredeck, and stepped through the open hatch into the control room. He walked up to the chief officer and said, "Sir, we have a breached container."

"Secure it, immediately."

"Aye, sir."

The seaman left the control room and went down a short flight of metal stairs where the uppermost containers were stored just below the observation deck. A door with 345 in bold numerals was hanging open on a blue sea van. He edged his way over and grabbed hold of a steel rung to look inside.

An army of centipedes stormed out, slamming him up against the bulkhead. The ones that weren't devouring the sailor were racing over the cargo containers and up the metal stairs to the observation deck. They charged through the open hatch and invaded the bridge.

The captain was in the middle of making an adjustment on a control panel when he was savagely attacked. He fell back into a bookcase. Maritime manuals hit the deck as the creatures bored into him.

The chief officer tried to run, but they were too fast, and he, too, suffered the same fate.

Hordes of centipedes quickly took over the ship, racing down each deck in a murderous spree, killing the cook and his mate in the galley, the men in the crew's mess, and eventually, those in the engine room and the other compartments.

The *Far Horizon* had become a ghost ship in only a matter of minutes.

***

Jeremiah was nearly to the top spire of the south tower when he finally ran out of paint. He straddled his feet on the wide cable and took a moment to take in the spectacular view. Few people ever got this opportunity. To him, it was a privilege to be up here; a similar feeling one might experience after climbing Mt. Everest. Only he got to do this every day.

He had the perfect seat whenever Navy aircraft carriers and other warships passed under the bridge during Fleet Week. He often felt like he could reach up and touch the underbellies of the

Blue Angels as the tight formation squadron of F/A-18 Hornets flew by.

Jeremiah got a sick feeling in his stomach when he looked down and saw a cargo container ship about a quarter-mile away. Instead of being in the middle of the channel where the water was the deepest, the ship seemed to be steering toward the platform supporting the south tower. It was definitely off course, and he knew if that vessel with all that weight were to plow into the stanchion, it would severely damage the bridge.

He shouted and waved his arms even though he knew it was futile. No one on the ship was going to see or hear him. In fact, he didn't even see anyone on the observation deck, which was odd, as there should at least be lookouts with binoculars.

He could feel that vacuous feeling in his gut; something he had never felt since working on the bridge, and that was genuine fear.

The giant monstrosity came under the span.

Jeremiah grabbed his lifeline cables with both hands, and closed his eyes, expecting the bridge to shuddered, as the hull rammed the concrete pillar and buckled the steel structure, causing the roadway to collapse and sending drivers to their doom while metal and concrete crashed down into the water, as he fell from the cable, his only thought as he plummeted, that he should have listened to his wife and friends, and changed his profession, but now it was too late.

But none of that had happened when he opened his eyes.

The container ship had miraculously drifted back on course and was heading out into the Pacific Ocean.

CHAPTER FORTY-FIVE

Four weeks later…

Jake sat on the couch with his bare feet on the coffee table. A large rectangular box was on the floor. Across the room, a muted 60-inch high-definition TV was turned on, but the picture was extremely letterboxed. He studied the user manual in hopes of better understanding the instructions for the remote control.

Nora came in from the kitchen carrying sandwiches on two plates. She nudged Jake's feet off, and placed the plates on the coffee table. She went back into the kitchen and returned with two bottles of beer.

She sat down next to her husband and handed him a bottle.

"Thanks."

"Any luck figuring out our new toy?"

Jake turned a page on the user manual. "I'm getting there."

Nora looked at the screen and saw a man wearing foul weather gear with a microphone, standing on a rocky beach in the pouring rain. A stormy ocean was in the background, white-capped with rough swells while heavy waves crashed onto the shore.

"What are you watching?" she asked.

"I don't know," Jake replied, staring down at the pamphlet. "The SyFy channel, I think."

The camera angle moved to the left of the reporter so the audience could view the cargo container ship listing on its side, having run ashore on a jetty of boulders and spilling thousands of different-colored cargo containers into the sea, most of them still afloat.

"Can you turn it up?" Nora asked.

Jake pressed the volume button on the remote.

"Last night, during the peak of Hurricane Madeline, the cargo container ship, *Far Horizon*, was dashed against these rocks that you see behind me. Rescue boats are in the water, but so far, there has been no sign of the crew, and it is feared that they have all perished. This is by far, the worst shipwreck in this part of the hemisphere, in the past decade," the reporter's voice boomed.

Pickup trucks were racing across the sand, men holding rifles, standing in the cargo beds. Hundreds of impoverished-looking people were running into the water to salvage what they could from the wreckage.

"As you can see behind me, there is bedlam here as the locals try to scavenge whatever they can get their hands on." Machinegun fire erupted off camera and the reporter flinched. "To make matters worse, some of the warlords and their men have arrived. The situation here is about to get extremely dangerous."

A voice off camera muttered something.

"I'm sorry," the reporter said. "We seem to be having…"

A small group of frightened people ran away from the shoreline. Three men with guns were firing their weapons.

Jake looked up. "I don't remember seeing this."

"Must be a new release," Nora said, leaning closer to watch.

A glitch etched across the screen as if the cameraman was experiencing some type of problem with his equipment.

"Jesus, what are those things?" the reporter screamed. He turned and faced the camera. "Emerson, watch out, behind you!"

The reporter dropped his microphone and ran off screen.

Jake glanced down at the user manual. "Oh, here it is. It's the aspect ratio setting." He used the remote to guide him to a menu screen, selected the appropriate setting for full screen, and pressed the button to return to their program.

"Oh my God," Nora said, when she saw the giant twenty-foot-long centipedes chasing the people down the beach in marvelous high-definition on their new big screen TV and everyone was screaming at the top of their lungs in glorious surround sound.

Jake stared at the screen. "I can't believe it."

"Me neither," Nora said. "It's only been a month and already it's a movie?"

THE END

CPSIA information can be obtained
at www.ICGtesting.com
Printed in the USA
LVOW11s1015170417
531084LV00001B/71/P